THE DISAPPEARING DINOSAUR

ADVENTURE • NET
#3
THE DISAPPEARING DINOSAUR

Andrea and David Spalding

Whitecap Books

Edited by Carolyn Bateman
Proofread by Elizabeth McLean
Cover design by Roberta Batchelor
Cover illustration by Lorna Bennett
Interior design by Antonia Banyard

Readers are welcome to
contact the authors at
andreas@gulfislands.com
or via Whitecap Books at
whitecap@whitecap.ca

Printed in Canada

National Library of Canada Cataloguing in Publication Data

Spalding, Andrea.
  The disappearing dinosaur

  (Adventure.net ; #3)
  ISBN 1-55285-311-X

  I. Spalding, David A. E., 1937– II. Title. III. Series: Adventure net ; #3
PS8587.P213D57 2002   jC813'.54   C2002–910196–4
PZ7.S7319Di 2002

The publisher acknowledges the support of the Canada Council for the Arts
and the Cultural Services Branch of the Government of British Columbia
for our publishing program. We acknowledge the financial support of the
Government of Canada through the Book Publishing Industry Development
Program for our publishing activities.

For Tosh — a young dinosaur devotee.

ACKNOWLEDGMENTS

No book is completed without a diversity of help from relatives, friends, and colleagues. Our daughter Penny Spalding read drafts and shared her memories of visiting dinosaur digs as a child. Eleven-year-old dinosaur enthusiast Nick Wilde also read outlines and drafts and made helpful comments. Dave's dentist, Dr. Babin, provided a (relatively) restful environment in his chair in which to develop plot ideas, while Tyrrell technician Darren Tanke told Dave the true story of the left-handed sardine cans. George Melnyk and Julia Berry offered accommodation and encouragement while we were doing fieldwork for the project.

Our editor, Carolyn Bateman, and the staff at Whitecap all contributed notably as we moved from original idea to completed book. And no series is complete without its readers, who give us helpful suggestions and tell us that they can't wait to read the next one.

CHAPTER ONE

"Are we there yet?" asked Rick Forster.

The bright blue school bus with the leaping orca painted on the side droned across the Alberta prairie. Endless fields of ripening grain shimmered in the heat of the August sun. Marty Forster took his eyes off the road for a second and glanced over at his son. Rick was slumped in the front seat, his bent head and dark spiky hair almost hiding his palm-sized computer game.

"You don't seem very interested in the scenery, Rick."

Rick grinned and waved a hand dismissively. "Aw, come on, Dad. It's flat. Seen one kilometre, seen 'em all. Tell me when we get to the dinosaur." He went back to his game.

Marty fumbled in a file stuffed beside the driver's seat and pulled out a sheet of paper. "Actually, I could do with some help. Are you up to some map reading?"

"Sure." Rick sat up, looking interested. "Have we finally arrived?"

His dad nodded. "Almost, but we need to find the field

7

camp before the light goes. What's the name of the little town we're looking for?"

Rick peered at the map sketched on a scrap of paper. "Dry Valley."

"It should be coming up in the next couple of clicks. Watch for it."

"There's grain elevators up ahead," said Rick. "That must be it. Yeah, there's the sign."

As they approached the junction, Marty slowed down, flicked on the indicator, and turned the bus onto a gravel road. It lurched from pothole to pothole and its wheels spun up clouds of dust. The computer game flew onto the floor, and Rick banged his head on the side window.

"Whoa. What's with the rock and roll?" Rick grumbled.

"Just a rough patch of gravel. Better get used to it. The roads are even worse in the badlands."

Rick stared with interest as they slowly bounced through the small community of Dry Valley.

"Dry Valley, the middle of nowhere," announced Rick. "Willow's gonna love this."

Marty chuckled. "Your sister has definitely enjoyed being in the big city for a change. But we're here for the dinosaurs, not the decor. I'm sure she'll enjoy those too."

Main Street was barely a block long. Two elevators stood beside the single railroad track. They drove past a garage and a Chinese restaurant, followed by a general store with a sagging veranda. A rusty tin sign showing an ice cream cone waved sluggishly in the dusty breeze. A large hardware store and a square wooden hotel completed the scene. On the side opposite the tracks, several small roads ran off at right angles and passed through a cluster of houses. All around, the fields stretched out in a golden sweep to the far horizon.

"So where's the valley?" asked Rick, as they passed the last houses minutes later.

"See that dip in the road just ahead?" said Marty. "I guess that's it. The dig's along the coulee somewhere."

Rick checked the map and directed Marty to turn the bus up a track. They passed a farm, then wandered along a series of steadily deteriorating tracks between the fields.

"We've lost the valley again," Rick said. "I'm just seeing prairie. Maybe we should have asked at the farm?"

As Rick spoke, Marty noticed a small sign leaning against a fence. It showed a crudely sketched dinosaur and an arrow pointing toward a side track across the fields. The track dipped and the bus was suddenly running in a steadily deepening, almost invisible rift below the rim of the prairie. The coulee was narrow and winding and the driving became tricky in the evening light. They rounded a bluff and Marty halted the bus.

Before them stretched a wide valley filled with badlands — hundreds of hummocky hills of yellow-brown rock with bands of darker brown rock striped across them. The setting sun flamed the tops of the hills with red.

"It's a Martian landscape," gasped Rick.

Little grew in this harsh desert valley except an occasional sage bush and some small patches of cactus. The one touch of green was a distant thin line of cottonwood trees beside the river that wandered through the centre far below.

The trail ahead forked, with one branch continuing down the gully and the other climbing up another steep bluff. A jeep was parked on the top, silhouetted against the sunset. Marty pointed. "That must be near the dig. Let's go and make ourselves known."

He let out the clutch and the bus trundled slowly along the ridge.

The empty jeep was parked beside a large outcrop of rock, and Marty parked the bus beside it. Marty climbed out of the bus, stretched, and ran both hands through his dark curly hair while he gazed at the view. Rick headed straight for the rock and cautiously peered over the cliff edge.

"Dad. There's a rope." As Marty joined him, Rick pointed out where it was knotted around the rock and lay over the cliff. Suddenly it jerked and they heard scrabbling sounds below.

"Hello?" Marty called down.

"Hi there. You must be Marty and Rick. Step back, I'm coming up." A thirty-something man with a small dark beard and a floppy hat waved, then began to haul himself up the cliff using the rope. He soon appeared over the rim and flashed a white grin.

Marty helped him over the edge.

"Thanks. I'm Doug Wong, chief technician at the Royal Tyrrell Museum. I'm in charge of the dig." He slapped some

Imagine you are a pioneer crossing the rolling grass-covered prairies of western North America. Suddenly your way is blocked by a bizarre landscape — a river valley full of strange rock formations. If you venture down into the narrow, twisting gullies, you would soon lose your way among rocks, hillocks and hoodoos, mounds, and mesas. French voyageurs called these areas *mauvaises terres* — "bad lands." Pioneer settlers saw no reason to change the name. The bare ground wasn't much use for grazing cattle and could not be plowed.

But when fossil hunters came west, they found that erosion of these areas of bare rock exposed many ancient bones. Fossil collectors have learned to seek them out, to study them, and know them intimately. Today, paleontologists visit them to find dinosaurs and other fossils. If they had come first, we might now know these areas as "goodlands."

You can visit badlands in southern Saskatchewan (Grasslands National Park) and along the Red Deer River in Alberta, especially in Dinosaur Provincial Park. Many other areas are found in the U.S., especially in the Dakotas (Badland's National Monument) and other western states.

http://parkscanada.pch.gc.ca/unesco/DINO/Dino_e.htm

sand from his hands and shook theirs. "Glad you could make it."

"Hey, we're glad to be here," said Marty. "I'm just sorry we're so late, but I had to make another call on the way. I tried phoning this afternoon but lost the line."

"Yup. Cellphones don't always work in the dead areas of the badlands. The temporary line at base camp works fine, but there was no one there until a couple of hours ago. We don't run to an answering machine," Doug explained.

Marty looked at his watch. "Can we go to the base camp now so we know where it is? I've got to head out again. My daughter was finishing a dance course in Calgary today, so my wife, Shari, stayed with her. It meant she could pick up the edited tape the last filmmaker shot and bring it with her. They're coming in to Dry Valley on the evening bus."

"I've got news for you," said Doug. "You can relax. Your wife phoned an hour ago. The tape wasn't ready, so she's arriving tomorrow." He looked across at Rick, who was poking the rope with the tip of his shoe. "Don't mess with that rope, Rick. It's already wiped out one team member."

"Was this where the filmmaker fell? The one that Dad's replacing?"

"Yeah. Now the gang calls this spot Deeley's Dive." Doug gave an uncomfortable laugh.

"Poor old Bill," said Marty. "I still haven't been able to thank him for putting you on to me. It's not like him to be so careless."

"Wasn't his fault — the rope came loose somehow," Doug said. "But don't worry, it won't happen again."

12

"I could climb down without the rope," said Rick, peering down the cliff.

"You don't usually have to climb down," said Doug. "We hike in to the site along the coulee bottom. But that's a long way to haul heavy equipment, so we run it up here and lower it over with the truck winch."

Rick pointed to the ledge at the bottom of the cliff, which was littered with tools and tarps. "Is that the *Tyrannosaurus rex* dig? Can I go down and see it?"

Doug Wong squinted at the sunset. "Not this evening. The light's about to go. It'll get dark as soon as the sun drops below the valley rim and it's almost sunset now. Let's get you to the camp. I'll show you the dig tomorrow. Follow me."

The jeep and the bus bumped slowly down the track and turned down the coulee into a maze of badlands.

Doug was right. Within a few minutes, the brilliant orange sunset had dissolved into a grey twilight with disorienting heavy shadows cast from the towering hummocks. Marty crouched over the wheel, manoeuvring the bus around tight corners, and following the jeep's tail lights. He sighed with relief when the trail widened out and they drove into a circle of trailers, cars, and a rabble of tents. Doug leaned out of the jeep window and pointed to a large empty space at the far end.

Marty gave a thumbs-up and parked the bus. He and Rick climbed out and looked around curiously.

They were on a wide flat area not far from the river. Behind them towered the bewildering maze of badlands, but the base camp area seemed cozy and friendly. A utility trailer, obviously the kitchen, was parked on one side of the circle. There was a faint background hum of a generator, and a string of lights ran from the trailer to a small stand of cottonwood trees. They cast a friendly glow over a cluster of picnic

>>>>>>> **The Royal Tyrrell Museum** <<<<<<

 In 1985, one of the world's finest dinosaur museums opened in the badlands, near the town of Drumheller, Alberta. It was named after geologist Joseph Burr Tyrrell, who had found the first *Albertosaurus* nearly a century before. After a visit from Queen Elizabeth II in 1990, it became one of the few museums in Canada entitled to call itself "Royal."

The museum shows the entire fossil history of western Canada but gives particular emphasis to the wonderful dinosaur record of Alberta's badlands. Its dinosaur hall contains more than 50 skeletons and casts, making it one of the biggest dinosaur museums in the world.

The museum staff runs important research programs and studies dinosaurs and other fossils in China and Argentina as well as Canada. Many volunteers work on the museum's digs in the badlands. You might see — or even take part in — a dig if you visit the Tyrrell.

www.tyrrellmuseum.com/

tables. But the tables were empty. Everyone was sitting around a blazing campfire eating bowls of what smelled like chili.

Rick sniffed hungrily. He was suddenly ravenous.

Doug beckoned them over.

"Everyone. This is Marty Forster, our new cameraman, and his son, Rick."

"Hi guys," said Marty. "My wife, Shari Jennings, will be working on the film too. She'll be along tomorrow with Rick's sister."

"She's called Willow," added Rick.

Shadowy figures called out a variety of greetings and waved to them.

"I know you won't remember everyone's names," continued Doug. "But Rick, this is Heather." A slim older woman with short grey hair and glasses waved her spoon at him. "She's a volunteer who's come over from England to help us excavate. She'll look after you when you're on the dig. If you need anything when I'm busy, ask her."

Rick gave a small, embarrassed nod.

"Wally and Jimmy are on Heather's left. They've left their studies for the summer and come across the border to show us how to dig. They're the muscles in this operation."

Two young college students — Wally broad, bushily bearded, and grinning; Jimmy tall, lanky, and clean-shaven — flexed their arms and grunted.

"He's the muscles, I'm the brains," Jimmy added with a sour expression, pointing to Wally with his thumb.

Everyone laughed.

15

"Luisa is a trainee preparator," continued Doug, indicating a tall girl in black. "She's on exchange from Spain. Ask her about the Costa del Dinosaurios." Luisa smiled shyly.

"We call the big guy over there Herman, but in town they call him Dr. Muller, 'cause he's the Dry Valley dentist. He excavates here when he's not excavating the locals' teeth."

Chuckles ran around the campfire.

"There'll be temporary volunteer help too, especially at weekends. They'll come and go, so you'll learn their names gradually. But don't hesitate to ask the volunteers anything. They know nearly as much as the staff."

Cries of "More, Doug … definitely more," echoed round the campfire.

Doug chuckled. "Last but not least is Charlie, our cook. Be nice to her. She's the most important person on the team. Tick her off, and we don't eat."

Charlie, a plump young woman in a stained white apron, put on a fierce scowl and waved a ladle in a threatening manner. Then she laughed. "Nobody's missed a meal yet. Come and join us. There's plenty."

Rick looked around happily. This was amazing. He'd been interested in dinosaurs for as long as he could remember. Now he was in a field camp run by the famous Tyrrell Museum, and tomorrow he'd get the chance to dig for a real dinosaur.

Doug seemed to read Rick's mind. He clapped Rick and Marty on the shoulders. "You'll meet Vicky in the morning."

"Who's Vicky?" asked Rick.

A gale of laughter swept around the campfire.

Doug punched the air with delight. "Yes! Our campaign of secrecy is working. They didn't know!" He turned to Rick and Marty with enthusiasm. "Vicky's our dinosaur. What we hope will be the most exciting *T. rex* skeleton ever found. The locals know there's a *T. rex* dig here, but they think it's just a few bones. Only those of us working on her know how special Vicky is."

"Gotta fill out a form to say you'll keep the secret until we give you permission," called out Wally, fingering his beard.

"Gotta sign it in blood," added Jimmy without cracking a smile.

Rick's excitement grew. What could be more exciting than a *Tyrannosaurus*? "Is Vicky complete like that really famous *T. rex* called Sue? Does she have a skull?" he asked.

There was a doleful silence.

"Not quite," said Doug slowly. "We think we know where it might be, and we're hoping to locate it before the dig is closed down next week. It's going to be a close call and we'd love to have it … so keep your fingers crossed."

Rick held up his hands to show all eight fingers crossed. The crew chuckled.

"Hmm. I'm good at finding things," Rick thought to himself. "Maybe *I'll* be able to help find the *T. rex* skull."

CHAPTER TWO

Rick woke to brilliant sunshine and silence. No birds, no traffic, no one moving around the converted school bus that his family called home for much of the year. He blinked sleepily and gathered his thoughts together. Ah, yes! He was in the middle of the badlands. He had sat up listening to the talk around the campfire about the famous collectors and their great discoveries. And now his parents were going to film a dinosaur dig, and maybe he would have his chance to discover fossils.

Rick rolled eagerly out of his bunk bed, found his jeans and T-shirt, made a sketchy visit to the tiny bathroom across the corridor, and erupted into the main living area of the converted school bus.

"Dad?" he called.

A note was prominently propped up on the table.

Didn't want to wake you. You definitely need your beauty sleep.

Rick grinned.

The dig started early, at 6 a.m. Check in with Charlie when you wake up. Someone will guide you to the site when you're ready. Mom and Willow will join us around 2 p.m.

Dad

Rick opened the fridge and swigged some milk from the carton. He poured the rest over some cereal, sliced a banana into it, and topped it off with a scoop of ice cream. He took the bowl outside into the sunshine.

"Hi," said a voice. "You must be Rick. I'm Victoria."

Rick turned toward the group of tables where a girl around twelve years old was sitting peeling an orange.

Victoria eyed his bowl enviously. "Do you always have ice cream for breakfast?"

Rick licked his lips. "Only when my parents aren't around."

"What's with the whale?" she asked, pointing to the bus.

"My parents' company is called Orca Enterprises," explained Rick, sitting down beside her. "They make films and teach moviemaking all over the place. So my sister and I live in the bus and travel around with Mom and Dad."

"So you do correspondence school, right?"

"Yes," said Rick.

"And you have a base in Vancouver for the winter."

"Who told you that?"

"And you take special classes when you get the chance."

"Hey, what is this?" said Rick.

If your grandfather and his brother, and your dad and his two brothers, all collected dinosaurs, what would you want to do for a living?

Charles Hazelius Sternberg was born in 1850 and moved with his family to Kansas, in the centre of the U.S. His elder brother was collecting fossils, and young Charles began to do the same — first leaves and then bones. While still a student, he was paid to collect by a leading dinosaur specialist, Edmund Cope. Sternberg collected all over North America, sending dinosaurs, marine reptiles, fish, and mammals to museums around the world.

His three sons, George, Charles Mortram, and Levi, all worked with him, becoming experts in their turn. The family came to Canada to collect for the Geological Survey, and the two younger sons stayed for the rest of their lives. Levi became chief technician at the Royal Ontario Museum in Toronto, while Charles Mortram became Canada's "Mr. Dinosaur" at Ottawa's national museum.

When Charles Mortram's son Ray joined him in the field in Dinosaur Provincial Park, he found and later described another new fossil, a bird that is now known to be a dinosaur. So three generations of the same family have contributed to the science of dinosaurs.

www.fhsu.edu/sternberg/family.html

"And when does Willow arrive?" added Victoria, smiling. Rick stared at her. "Why? Do you know her?"

Victoria tossed her dark hair back over her shoulder. "We both took the same dance course in Calgary. Yesterday she told me you guys were coming out here. That was a surprise."

"We only just found out," Rick said between crunchy mouthfuls.

"It's great," Victoria gushed. "Me and Willow are going to hang out together. After I've shown her my dinosaur."

Rick licked the last bit of ice cream off his spoon and looked at her curiously. "What do you mean 'your dinosaur'?"

"Vicky. She's named after me ... I found her."

Rick gazed at her speechlessly, then stuttered. "You ... you ... found the ... the *T. rex*? On your own?"

"Yup." Victoria got up from the table and carried her glass across to the kitchen trailer. She leaned inside. "Please can I have some more milk, Charlie?"

Charlie appeared in the doorway with a jug and refilled Victoria's glass. "Good morning, Rick. Want some?" She waved the jug in Rick's direction.

He lifted his hand in greeting but shook his head. "No thanks." He turned to look at the surrounding badlands. "Wow! I found a boulder full of silver in the Kootenay mountains, but a *T. rex*! That's unbelievable!" Rick gazed at Victoria in total admiration

"It was kinda cool," Victoria agreed. "I live up at the farm. I was dirt biking down the badlands, and the back wheel slid sideways and started a little avalanche. When I looked back, there was this awesome big bone sticking out of the hill. I told Mom and Dad, and they said I should phone the Tyrrell Museum. So I did. A curator came out to look at it and here it is next summer and we've got a dig going on our land … but it's top secret. Neat, eh?"

"Totally," breathed Rick. "Is the curator working on the dig?"

"Nope. He's on a dig in China. So Doug's been left in charge here."

Victoria finished her milk. "Are you done? I'll take you out to the dig if you're ready." She jammed a cowboy hat on her head. "Got a hat? You'll get sunstroke if you don't. We don't need more things going wrong or everyone will really freak. Oh, and we pick up drinks and lunches from Charlie."

"Give me a minute." Rick ran back to the bus. Dumping his bowl and banana peel in the galley sink, he grabbed his baseball cap, pulled it on backwards, then leaped down the bus steps. "Ta daa."

They waved to Charlie, picked up their lunches, then started to hike along the badland trail.

"Hey, Victoria. What did you mean about everyone freaking?" Rick asked curiously.

Victoria looked very mysterious. "I reckon this dig is like the one for King Tutankhamen. You know — the curse of the mummy's tomb." She laughed, then sobered. "It's the curse of the dinosaur's grave. All sorts of nasty things have happened."

"You mean like Bill Deeley breaking his leg?"

Victoria nodded. "Yeah … poor Bill. That was awful …

Children have made some important dinosaur discoveries. One well-known *T. rex* was found in Alberta in 1981 by three high school students, Jeff Baker, Peter Kosci, and Bradley Mercier. Its black-stained bones led the fossil to be nicknamed Black Beauty, and it became a centrepiece in the Dinosaur World Tour travelling exhibit.

Another southern Alberta teenager, Wendy Sloboda, was a high school student in 1987 when she discovered egg fragments, which led to the discovery of the first dinosaur nest in Canada. The world press was so excited that journalists spent a month following Wendy around while she led them everywhere but to the nest site. Her find resulted in protection of the Devil's Coulee nesting site in southern Alberta, and the creation of a museum in her hometown.

More recently, an important small dinosaur was discovered by schoolboy Wes Linster on his family's farm in Montana. He suggested the name of what is now known as *Bambiraptor*.

Besides dinosaurs, lots of other important fossil finds have been made by kids — from rare Precambrian plants to more familiar pterosaurs and plesiosaurs, and even giant pigs and early people.

www.bambiraptor.com/Pages/Intro.html

but listen to what else has gone wrong." She began to tick the items off on her fingers. "Small bones have gone missing ... important pieces that just vanished into thin air. And the map of the site disappeared from Doug's trailer."

"Aren't there other copies?" Rick was puzzled.

"No, this was the map Doug had drawn. The one showing how the bones are lying in the rock. It was gone for two days before it suddenly turned up again in the kitchen trailer. That was really strange! Doug was really upset when it got lost. He said it would take him a week to do a new one. When it turned up in the kitchen, Charlie thought everyone was blaming her. She was so mad she made liver and onions for supper two days running."

"Yuck! Gross," said Rick. They both made gagging sounds and laughed.

"Then the phone line went down, and the computer was sabotaged. The e-mail program still isn't working properly," Victoria continued. "Now Doug can't talk to other scientists who are also working on dinosaur digs. And the technician's on holiday, so they can't get it fixed."

"E-mail programs can go wrong all by themselves," Rick muttered.

Victoria continued as if he hadn't spoken. "Then the truck wouldn't work, and Charlie couldn't get into town for supplies. Doug thought it had been sabotaged too. But it was suddenly okay a day later ... weird, eh?"

Rick nodded.

"Finally, the rope slipped when Bill Deeley was hanging

24

over the dig, filming." She dropped her voice. "I think someone did it on purpose. I tell you, this dig is cursed."

"Don't you think it could all be coincidence?" Rick asked.

Victoria shook her head so hard her hat flew off and her hair bounced out in a mop and covered her face. She picked up her hat and jammed it on impatiently, tucking her hair inside. "I know it sounds nuts. But honestly, people are acting weird. I wish I knew why!"

"Have you told anyone?"

"Sure. I told Doug I thought all these things were connected, but he just laughed and said I was a drama queen." She glared at Rick, daring him to comment.

Rick stopped walking. "I don't want anything nasty to happen to Mom or Dad," he said. "We should try and find out if something is really going on."

"How?" said Victoria.

Rick looked uncertain. "By watching people? We can keep our eyes and ears open, and pool information."

Victoria grinned. "You mean hang out and spy?"

"Yeah. When Willow arrives she'll help," added Rick. "There'll be three of us. Maybe we can stop anything else going wrong."

Victoria gave a little skip of excitement. "Great. I've always wanted to be a secret agent. Let's talk about it later. Come on, we're nearly there."

They walked around the promontory of a big bluff and into a hive of activity.

Was Tut's tomb cursed?

 The tomb of ancient Egypt's boy king Tutankhamen was discovered in 1922. In the next few years, newspapers published many stories about a curse and the supposed early deaths of its discoverers.

The apparent curse "Death shall come on swift wings to him that touches the tomb of Pharaoh" was often quoted, yet no such inscription was found in the tomb. The story seems to have started when the sponsor of the excavation, Lord Carnarvon, died some months afterwards of pneumonia following an infected mosquito bite. Other people associated with the discoverers died in later years. But the 10 men present when the mummy was unwrapped were all still alive 11 years later.

No one knows if the journalists who wrote the stories believed what they wrote, but their editors obviously knew a good story when they saw one. Every time King Tut's tomb is in the news, the story surfaces again. New "scientific" explanations of the supposed deaths often appear — from bacteria or moulds from the mummy to radioactive radon gas.

Even more improbable stories have been widely believed. A Toronto newspaper once published an account of King Tut's golden typewriter!

www.powerup.com.au/~ancient/curse.htm

CHAPTER THREE

The dig was taking place near the top of the badlands where a natural ledge had been widened and deepened by cutting away the rock. A dozen people were working around several big, white, shapeless objects. Some were chipping or scraping at the rock, others wheeling away wheelbarrows of rubble or taking photos.

Marty was hanging over the top of the cliff, lying on his belly, filming it all. Rick waved both arms until he caught Marty's eye and he waved back.

Victoria scrambled up to the ledge with Rick following close behind her. He stood on the edge trying to make sense of what was happening.

Yellow-brown bones were exposed on the quarry floor. Rick recognized some of the team working on them. Doug was painting one large bone with what looked like varnish, and Heather was scraping, chipping, and brushing away rock chips beside another. Jimmy was at the back of the dig using a power drill to gouge into the cliff side, while Wally cleared up the rubble.

Tyrannosaurus rex is the best-known dinosaur of all, and for years it was considered the biggest of the predatory dinosaurs. Its name means "king tyrant lizard." *T. rex* is found in the northern United States and Canada and dates from the late Cretaceous, about 70 million years ago.

Mounted on two sturdy hind legs, *T. rex* walked with its body roughly horizontal. Its metre-long head had a mouthful of large pointed teeth. Its tiny forelegs were too short to reach the ground when it was standing, but were quite strongly built and might have been useful in holding prey or helping the animal get up from a lying position.

As research continues in other parts of the world, similar large carnivores are being discovered. *Tarbosaurus* from Mongolia, *Giganotosaurus* from Argentina, and *Carcharodontosaurus* from Morocco could be even larger.

www.ucmp.berkeley.edu/trex/trexpo.html

Doug stood up, rubbed his back, and strode over to them. "You finally made it. So, what do you think of Vicky? Isn't she beautiful?"

Rick chuckled. Beautiful wasn't quite the word he would have chosen. He tipped his head to one side, trying to make sense of the jumble of bones. "She's more like a giant jigsaw puzzle than a dinosaur."

"Exactly," Doug agreed enthusiastically. "You have to have dug here from the beginning before you can see her. We've uncovered a pile of pieces and have to remove them from the rock before we can put them together again." He waved his arms over his head to demonstrate. "The rock covered it all except for the slope over there. Isn't that right, Victoria?"

Victoria grinned. "Yup, that's where I came sliding down the hill on the bike, and loose rocks came away. Suddenly there was this big bone. Like this one." She pointed to the bone at Rick's feet. "A whopping great tailbone — a giant vertebra." Confidently, she picked up her tools and headed off to start scraping away at her bone. Rick watched enviously, wondering what he could do.

"I started out just like Victoria," said Doug, amused. "Just a kid on a bike in the badlands. Find a few bones, take a few exams, and here I am running a dinosaur dig."

But Rick was looking around thoughtfully. "So if the tail was over here … that must be the body in the middle …."

Doug nodded encouragement. "You've got it. We've already plastered the main part of the pelvis," he added, pointing to the shapeless mass looking like a giant marshmallow in the middle of the dig. "The smaller one contains some backbone and a portion of Vicky's ribs. We've freed them, then hardened and plastered them for protection. Now they're waiting till we can lift them out and take them to the museum by truck."

Dinosaur fossils are often found by accident. Children playing, farmers plowing, hikers and rockhounds in the badlands all find important specimens and report them to museums. Many more are found by a deliberate search. When paleontologists have time, they go out and explore likely areas. If possible, good fossil areas are checked every year because erosion reveals new specimens, especially after a major rainfall.

A dinosaur bone sticking out of the ground may be just one bone — or it may be the tip of an entire skeleton hidden in the rocks. After finding a bone, a paleontologist will look carefully for other small pieces that have eroded out of the rock and will gather them up before they are lost. A careful excavation around the bone will show what part of the body it is, perhaps what kind of dinosaur it belongs to, and if it is associated with other bones.

Specimens that are rare, in danger of damage from rapid erosion, and easy to extract are likely to be excavated first.

"Then is its neck going into the hillside?" asked Rick. "If so, the head should be that way," he finished, pointing triumphantly.

"You're a smart kid. That's where it would be if all of the skeleton is still together. But the neck of a dead dinosaur is always the weakest place. The head is heavy and may have broken off and been carried away by flood water. We might have trouble finding this one." Doug beckoned Rick to follow him, and they circled round the plastered bones to where Wally and Jimmy were labouring at the rock face.

Bushy-bearded Wally put down his wheelbarrow and took off his broad-brimmed hat. "Watch out, here comes the boss!" he yelled.

Jimmy turned off the drill, took off his tractor cap, and hunkered down to rest, wiping his arm over a sweat-covered brow. He was as careful in his movements as Wally was flamboyant.

In the sudden silence, Rick grinned at them and peered at the channel in the rock face. Dark brown knobs showed where several aligned vertebrae were running straight into the cliff. The drillers were cutting away the cliff above and behind the bones. "How long is the neck?" he asked.

Jimmy shrugged and turned his head away.

"I've counted the vertebrae," Wally said officiously. "There should be four more to go … if they're all here. So keep your fingers crossed that they are, and the doggone skull is at the end of them. If there's no sign of a skull in the next couple of days, we're skunked."

A frown crossed Doug Wong's face. "I'd rather you got these vertebrae properly exposed and hardened, guys, then we can get them plastered and out of the way. You know we can't count on finding the skull here. When they excavated Sue, they found her skull under her pelvis. Vicky's might not be here at all."

"Don't you even *think* that," Wally said arrogantly. "We're gonna find it."

"We'll keep looking," Jimmy added quietly. "We don't mind working overtime."

"Yeah," said Wally. "I'm determined to see Vicky up close — eyeball to eye socket." He picked up the drill and headed into the cliff, while Jimmy reached for the shovel.

There was an edgy tone to Wally's banter. Rick felt uncomfortable. He looked up at Doug, who shrugged and turned away.

He walked back toward the massive leg bones Victoria was now working on with Luisa and waited for Rick to join him again. "It would be great if we find the skull before we shut down for the winter. But it can wait until we reopen the dig again next year. Skulls are very important to paleontologists, but a skull is not what makes our Vicky so special."

Luisa watched and smiled as Doug explained. When he knelt down and shifted some small stones, she came over and helped him roll up a square of tarp covering a small section of rock. "It's this area." He pointed proudly to a haphazard group of small bones.

Rick crouched down and fingered a flat bone arching up. "Is this a rib?" he asked.

"Good for you," said Doug. He hunkered down too.

"But look beneath the rib," said Luisa, pushing her long dark hair away from her face.

Rick peered at the exposed bedrock. The surface was criss-crossed with smaller bones all jumbled together.

"Wow. These are little bones. They look like a Thanksgiving turkey."

"A turkey's pretty close, Rick. Birds are descended from small relatives of raptors like *T. rex*."

"But these can't be from a *T. rex*. Are they bones from the prey the *T. rex* was eating?"

"Good guess, Rick, but not quite right." Doug's eyes were dancing, and he was grinning from ear to ear. "These small bones are why this dig is a gigantic secret. We think they're a really young *T. rex*."

Rick gasped. "Vicky's baby?" He stuck out his finger and gently stroked one of the small bones.

"You got it," said Doug. "Other *T. rexes* have been found with bones that might have been young ones. But this is the very first *T. rex* found with one so young it has to be a baby. If our analysis is right, Vicky will be the world's most famous mother."

"Totally awesome," said Rick.

"And I'll be her famous finder," said Victoria, coming up behind Rick and posing for invisible flash cameras. "Thank you, thank you."

Doug chuckled. "Famous or not … digging time is short, so Rick, why don't you help Heather."

Heather looked up from where she was working and smiled, her face wrinkling round her grey eyes. She moved over and patted the rock beside her invitingly.

"Heather's working on Vicky's left femur. She'll show you what to do."

"Fantastic," said Rick. He squatted confidently beside Heather, ready to excavate the entire bone on his own.

She handed him gloves, a chisel, and a hammer.

"I've been saving this side for you," she said.

>>>>>>>>>>>>>>>> **Birds and dinosaurs** <<<<<<<<<<<<

The idea that birds and dinosaurs are closely related has been around for a long time, but it is only in the past few decades that most paleontologists have been convinced by the growing body of evidence.

Dinosaurs were once thought to be without the breastbone (the keeled bone that supports the white meat of the turkey) that is so important in flying birds as a base to attach the flying muscles. It has now been found in a number of dinosaurs. Small raptors (carnivorous dinosaurs resembling birds of prey) have very many features in common with early fossil birds such as *Archaeopteryx*.

All that was needed seemed to be evidence that some dinosaurs developed feathers (perhaps as insulation) before they were used in flight. Recent dinosaurs found in China have a featherlike covering over the bodies, and most paleontologists now think that birds are descended from — and indeed are — dinosaurs.

www.sciam.com/explorations/062397dino/powell.html

CHAPTER FOUR

Several hours later, Rick was sweating and tired, but still doggedly scraping rock from the side of the femur. He'd eaten his lunch, swallowed litres of water to combat the heat and the dust, slathered on tubes of sunblock to combat sunburn, and wafted away a persistent fly that kept landing on his nose. "This is real hard work," he grumbled to Heather, putting down his tools and sagging visibly.

Heather smiled and patted his shoulder. "Look how much we've done." She waved her hand over the area they had worked on.

The bone was nearly as long as Rick was tall. Rick had chipped and scraped a deep groove in the sandstone along its entire length. Heather had followed behind, delicately removing the remaining pieces of rock against the bone.

"I guess it is a lot. But my hands are getting blistered."

"We've nearly finished the entire femur. If we clean out the joint with the tibia, we're ready to start plastering. I bet Doug will let you help. Then we can dig underneath it and the whole bone can be lifted up without damage."

Rick's spirits lifted. That would be great. And Heather was right. They'd accomplished more than he'd realized.

>>>>>>>>>>>>>>>>>>>>> **Digging a dinosaur** «««««««

Digging out a big skeleton can take months. A camp has to be set up and a trail or road made to the site. Some dinosaurs are deeply buried, and then tonnes of rock may have to be shifted off the top before the bones are exposed.

The really careful work begins as the top surface of each bone is uncovered and the outlines of the skeleton gradually uncovered in the rock. The best skeletons are articulated (with all the bones still associated as they were when the dinosaur was alive).

The tops of the bones are first covered with tissue paper, then plaster of Paris and burlap. This hardens to form a strong cast that will protect the bone while it is being transported. (You might have had a broken limb wrapped in a cast to protect it while it healed.)

Then the excavators burrow underneath each section until they can roll the pieces over. More of the rock is removed to reduce the weight, then the other side is plastered. Only when the complete plaster jacket is hardened can the bones be transported.

www.muohio.edu/dragonfly/skeletons/dig.htmlx

"Come on. Time for a break from the sun," said Heather.

They abandoned their tools, clambered down from the ledge and walked around to the deep shade in a small canyon between two hillocks. They stretched out in the cool and rested their aching muscles.

Rick lay down, clasped his hands behind his head, and closed his eyes. The draining desert heat was exhausting.

Heather revived in the shade. She started chatting.

"You're exactly the same age as my grandson in England," Heather said wistfully. "He'd love it here. He's like you, mad keen on dinosaurs." She sighed. "I really miss him."

"You'll see him when you go back to England, won't you?" asked Rick.

Heather shook her head. "Unfortunately, my daughter and I have fallen out," she admitted. "She won't invite me or let him visit. So I can only write and send little gifts."

"That's a bummer," said Rick. "My grandma lives in B.C., in Nanaimo. We visit lots. And she e-mails me."

He closed his eyes again and drifted into a light doze.

A scraping sound disturbed him. He opened one eye. Heather was scratching around the floor of the little canyon.

"What are you looking for?" Rick asked.

"Bone shards," said Heather. "We can keep small loose surface bits. I'll send them to my grandson."

"That's nice," muttered Rick sleepily. "Maybe I'll find something. I'd love to discover something special … like a claw … or a tooth. That would really rock …" His voice trailed off as his eyes closed again.

"Wakey, wakey! Who do you think you are, Sleeping Ugly?"

The unexpected sound of Willow's voice made Rick's eyes fly open. He sat up groggily. Heather had gone and the shadows were deeper. He must have slept for some time.

Willow grinned at her brother and plonked down beside him. She was no longer in city clothes as he had last seen her. Her old jeans were stained at the knees, and her blonde hair was tied back out of her eyes. She wafted her hand backwards and forwards like a fan. "This place is wild, but it's really cooking."

"Have you seen the dig?"

"Yeah. Mom and I got here about half an hour ago. I've even chiselled a bit of rock, but it's hard work in this heat. Dad said to tell you they'll be knocking off soon. It's too hot."

"That's why they start so early." Rick laughed. "You won't believe it, Willow. The dig started at six this morning!"

"No way, José. I'm not going to dig all the time. Victoria and I are going to hang out at the farm to perfect our dance routine. Did she tell you her dad made a dance studio in the top of the barn? She has a barre, and a big mirror, and a music system, and everything."

"Wow, really exciting," said Rick flatly. "I can't wait." He crossed his eyes, dropped his lower jaw, and slapped the side of his face.

"She also has Internet access and said we could use it if we wanted. She's got some new games," Willow added slyly.

"Now you're talkin'," said Rick. "Dad says we can't use the

camp phone 'cause there's only one." He scrambled to his feet. "Come on. Race you to the dig."

Willow shot to her feet, and the two of them sped along the canyon and around the bluff.

"Oops," said Rick. He stopped, just short of tumbling into a wheelbarrow of debris being pushed to the discard pile by Jimmy.

"Watch it, brats." Jimmy glared at them.

They waited as Wally followed with a second load. "Better stay out of the way, or you'll get squished as flat as Vicky," he growled.

"I don't like them," Willow whispered.

"Yeah. They're weird," Rick agreed. He watched as the two students dumped their loads, then paused to cool down in the shade. Their muttered conversation echoed softly up the canyon, just reaching Rick's ears.

He tugged Willow's arm and leaned against the wall in the shadows. Willow did the same. "What's up?" she said.

Rick frowned. "Shhh. Pretend you're talking to me. I want to eavesdrop." He rolled his eyes in the direction of the two students.

Willow caught on fast. She leaned against the wall and mimed whispering in his ear.

Jimmy had bent his tall frame to speak close to Wally's ear, and Rick strained in vain to hear.

Suddenly Jimmy straightened and spoke loudly and

angrily. "You're sure it's there, but I'm not. The line of vertebrae stops, so the damn skull's broken off. We might find it in the next five minutes, or it might be a pile of mud at the bottom of Lake Winnipeg. What *will* we do if we can't find it?"

Wally scratched his bearded chin. "We'll find it. Take it easy. Once we find it, we can start counting greenbacks."

"I'm not counting any chickens," Jimmy responded morosely.

"Then count dinosaurs. Wish she had two skulls. Then them dollars would really start talkin'."

"We'll never find one skull if we don't keep looking," grunted Jimmy. "Come on."

They picked up the wheelbarrows and trundled them past Rick and Willow, who were laughing maniacally as though they'd just shared the joke of the century.

"What was all that about?" whispered Willow. "Are you trying to find out who's put a curse on the dig?" Her eyes crinkled with laughter. "Are you?"

"Did Victoria tell you about it?" Rick asked.

Willow nodded. "Of course. It's all she talked about after Bill Deeley broke his leg while she was home for the weekend. You don't believe in a curse, do you?"

Rick shook his head. "Not really, but it sure sounds like something odd is happening. I figured if we listened and watched people when they were off on their own, we might find out what's going on."

"Those two didn't say much," said Willow.

"Nooo," Rick answered, hesitating. "But why are they talking about money? No one is selling Vicky. She's going to the Tyrrell Museum!"

The working day was over, but supper wasn't ready yet. Wally and Jimmy left the camp and strolled over the badlands to a little perch on the cliff, a private spot they used every afternoon where they could talk in private. Wally stubbed his toe on the rough ground and swore softly as they sat down.

"Got to keep an eye on those new kids," Jimmy grumbled. "What were they laughing at this afternoon? I didn't see anything funny."

"Who knows," answered Wally. "Kids is kids. They're just having fun."

"I'd have given my back teeth to work on a dig at their age. Think they heard what we were talking about?" continued Jimmy anxiously.

"What were we talking about?" asked Wally. "Relax. Nobody knows."

"Money. You say too much when people are around."

"So, they'll just think I'm funny about money. Wait till we get our hands on a dollar or two. What you gonna do with your share?"

"Pay my debts and finish grad school, like all these richy-ditchy kids spending daddy's money. I'll never get to the top without a doctor to my name. Tuck the rest away in a bank account somewhere offshore."

Most dinosaur digs are run by museums or universities. The person in charge of a museum dig usually stays with it from beginning to end. He or she may be a curator or a technician. A curator is in charge of a collection and to run a dinosaur dig would normally be a paleontologist (someone who studies fossils) or a geologist (an expert in rocks). A technician collects and prepares fossils and has expertise not only in fossils but in the methods and techniques needed.

Other staff on the dig might include junior curators and technicians, field assistants (who are hired for the summer), and other museum staff interested in having the experience. The rest of the team is normally made up of volunteers. These may include staff from other institutions, or they may be paleontology or geology students or interested amateurs from around the world who have taken a course or read enough about fossils to want to try their hand.

Some museums run digs almost entirely staffed by volunteers and even run digs where visitors can pay to join in for a day or longer. Some provide educational digs for school students.

www.isgs.uiuc.edu/dinos/dig.html

"You gotta think big," Wally grumbled. "Grad school's just the first step. I'm gonna get a proper field vehicle. Custom design, four-by-four, crew cab, extra-power winch, top of the line. Then I'm after big stuff. Sauropods. Got a cousin in the media — I can make my name with my own TV series."

"I'd like to break some new scientific ground. Hear Doug sound off about his visit to China this morning? That's where I'd like to be. All those feathered dinosaurs. Must be other new stuff coming out."

Wally guffawed. "Now you're talking. We'll both go. Crack me another can and we'll toast the first dinosaur expedition ever paid for by another dinosaur!"

"But we've got to have the skull," Jimmy added. "Your brother said it was essential. Otherwise no deal with this client."

"Yeah. I'd better get out and phone him this evening. See if the big man has confirmed the deal. Time for grub."

CHAPTER FIVE

Rick and Willow were cleaning up at the end of the afternoon as Shari bustled over. She pulled off her cap with the Kaslo film school logo and wiped her sweaty brow.

Rick eyed the new hairstyle with a grin. "Like the red spikes, Mom," he said.

She laughed. "If you can do it, so can I. Are you guys hiking back to base camp with the crew, or do you want to wait for us? We're going to catch some establishing shots of the badlands, but we should be finished in half an hour." She took a tube of skier's sunblock out of her pocket and drew a green stripe across her nose and cheeks. She offered it to Willow and Rick, but they both grinned and stepped back in mock horror.

"I'd like to look around for a bit," said Rick. "You know, explore the coulees. I haven't had time yet."

Willow was opening her mouth to protest when Victoria bobbed up from behind Shari. "Hang out with me," she said brightly. "I'll show you the way through the badlands back to my farm." She looked up at Shari. "Is it okay? My mom's invited them, and our farm's just up on the prairie. You passed it on the way in."

"I don't have a problem with that, do you, Marty?" Shari asked.

Marty shook his head as he fiddled with the tape casing in the camera. "There, got it. Ready, Shari?"

"Ready." Shari made an instant decision. "Okay, we'll pick you up from the farm before supper." She and Marty shouldered both cameras, but then Shari looked back. "Willow, where's your hat?"

Willow rolled her eyes, pulled a head scarf out of her pocket, and resentfully tied it around her hair. "Hats give me a headache," she argued.

Shari pulled a face and shook a finger in warning, then followed Marty along the base of the cliff.

By this time, Jimmy, the last of the crew, had left for camp, and the dig was deserted.

"Finally." Victoria spread her arms and danced around. "All three of us here and no adults. Now we can plan our spying campaign. Have you discovered anything, Rick?"

"Only that Wally and Jimmy are bothered that Vicky is worth less money without her skull."

"That's weird," said Vicky. "Who cares what it's worth? It's going to the Tyrrell Museum."

"That's what I said to Willow. What about you? Did you see or hear anything odd?" asked Rick.

"Yup ... Heather!"

"Heather!" exclaimed Rick. "What's she done? She talks a lot, but she's really nice!"

"Well, while you were sleeping, she came back to the dig looking guilty and stuffing something in her pocket," said Victoria.

Rick laughed. "She's collecting bone scraps. There's loads in the canyon. She's taking them back to her grandson in England. Come and see." Rick led the way to where he'd dozed and pointed out a few fragments on the ground.

"We can keep these?" asked Willow, suddenly interested. She knelt down and picked up a piece.

"Yeah. I've got lots," said Victoria. "They're all over the badlands. Doug says they're too small to identify so they're no use to the paleontologists." She looked puzzled. "But, if Heather was just collecting these, why did she look guilty?"

"Dunno." Rick shrugged.

Victoria looked excited. "Maybe she's our dinosaur thief and she's taken some more small bones."

Rick laughed. "Or maybe she fell asleep like I did and was embarrassed she'd taken such a long break."

Victoria looked crestfallen. "Nobody to spy on now," she said.

She led the way round the bluff and up a faint trail away from the main route to the camp. Victoria and Willow chatted and Rick kept his eyes on the ground.

"I wish I could find something really special," said Rick, picking up another bone scrap and cradling it in his hand. "I'd love to have a claw, or a vertebra, or a tooth. Those bits we found are nothing really. They're too tiny." He scuffed another bone fragment disparagingly with his foot. "But if these have all washed down from the walls of the badlands, I'm going to look higher up."

Rick scrambled up the steep slope like a monkey. Then he started raking the surface with his eyes. "I have a feeling about this," he murmured to himself. "The weirdest feeling ..."

The ground was covered with shattered pieces of dark brown rock and more tiny scraps of bone. But it was hard to keep his balance on the steep slope. The loose surface broke away under his feet. He slithered backwards across the face of the slope, showering debris down on the girls. "Rick, quit it!" yelled Willow. "Those rocks hurt."

Rick jammed one foot into a crack, grasped a protruding knob of rock with one hand, and finally stopped sliding. As he lay spread-eagled across the slope, with his nose almost in the dirt, he realized he was looking at a biggish chunk of broken bone with a distinctive edge. He picked it up, raised his head, and looked further up the slope. There was another loose piece. It looked as though it might match up with the first piece. He struggled back up the hill and examined the new find. It also had an interesting shape and had the same pattern on one edge. He sucked in his breath with excitement. Then, stuffing the pieces in his pocket, he looked around for more. His movement made part of the unstable surface shift again.

"Come down, you nut," called Willow.

No way was Rick leaving. He'd spotted another, much

Who owns fossils?

Some fossils, like the shells that are found in many limestones, are common, easy to collect, and of little scientific importance because scientists have already studied many of them. Others, like *T. rex* skeletons, are extremely rare and of great scientific value. Each new specimen gives new evidence that will help understand this great predator.

Scientists are not the only ones interested in fossils. Many people like to see fossils in museums and collect specimens for themselves. Some buy and sell them to make money. Important fossils are sometimes lost to science, collected illegally, stolen, smuggled into other countries, and even faked.

In many countries, governments make laws to protect fossils so they can be studied and exhibited for everyone's benefit. The laws determine who may collect them and where, and often prevent them being taken to another country. In Alberta, for instance, fossils belong to the provincial government and may only be excavated by experienced professionals with a permit.

www.tyrrellmuseum.com/Research_Resources/ Historical%20Resources/hra1.html

bigger piece of the same stuff just within reach. This piece was smooth and brown and its serrated edge glinted temptingly in the sunlight. It was almost as big as his hand. Excitedly, Rick stretched, grasped it, and pulled. But it remained firmly embedded in the rock. He pulled again. But his movement was too vigorous.

"Watch out, I'm slipping!" he yelled.

The girls leaped for safety as, with a roar, Rick and a pile of loose rock slid into the canyon.

Rick landed on the ground with a yelp and a thud. He lay still, his face planted squarely on a large slab of rock.

Willow ran over. "Rick. You okay?"

Rick groaned and lifted his head. Blood ran from his lip and a deep cut across his cheek.

Victoria screamed. "Help! Help! There's been another accident." She charged out of the canyon waving her arms and yelling at the top of her lungs. "Mr. Forster, Mr. Forster! HELP! Where are you? Rick's hurt. The curse of the dinosaur's grave is happening again!"

CHAPTER SIX

Rick lay in the dentist's chair. "I can't believe I did this," he thought, pressing an ice pack against his scraped face and puffy lip. "I never fall!"

The Dry Valley doctor had stitched up his cheek and lip and given him a tetanus injection. Now he was in the office of Dr. Muller, the dentist they'd met in the camp.

Dr. Muller squinted through little lenses attached to his glasses and gently probed Rick's tooth and the surrounding gum. Rick closed his eyes.

"The damage isn't as bad as it feels," said Dr. Muller eventually. "You chipped one corner of your front tooth on the rock. It's a little loose, but I think it'll tighten up on its own." He raised the chair so Rick could sit up. "You'll be fine. Just take it easy until the swelling goes down. No steak, but tell Charlie you can have lots of milkshakes."

His face was numb with the local anaesthetic, but Rick managed a weak, lopsided grin.

"Want to see a dentist's dream?" added Dr. Muller. He reached up to a shelf and lifted down a dark brown tooth the length of Rick's forearm. "Imagine getting a toothache in that, eh?"

Rick's eyes widened. He held out his hands.

Dr. Muller placed the tooth in them. "It's a *T. rex* tooth," he said proudly.

Rick stared. He ran his fingers over the edge of the tooth. It had two sharp edges serrated like a steak knife. He tried to form his words properly. "I 'ound thome pietheth 'ike thith'."

Luckily, Dr. Muller was used to his patients mumbling. "You found some pieces of tooth? Near the dig site?"

Rick nodded. "'en I fell."

"Has Doug seen them?"

Rick shook his head.

"Then you should show him. He'll want to check them out in case they're fragments from Vicky's skull."

Rick's eyes widened. He hadn't thought of that.

"Wait here. I'll see if your dad's in the waiting room."

Rick turned the *T. rex* tooth over. It was the biggest, most wicked tooth he'd ever seen. The chewing edges were still sharp. He could imagine the dinosaur tearing and chomping its prey. He fiddled in his pocket and pulled out one of the pieces he'd found and compared it.

His fragment was obviously from a smaller tooth, but it showed a bit of serrated edge like Dr. Muller's tooth.

"Maybe it's from the *T. rex* we're excavating," thought Rick with a flicker of excitement. "Shoot. That'll mean I can't keep it." He stowed the fragment in his pocket and enviously eyed Dr. Muller's tooth. "I wish this was mine."

He imagined it as the highlight of his rock and mineral collection. The current prize was a chunk from the gigantic silver boulder he'd helped to find in the Kootenay mountains. But this tooth was even more spectacular. He was wondering how the dentist had got hold of it. "He couldn't have ripped it off somewhere," thought Rick, remembering Victoria's tale of the missing bones. "Or he wouldn't show me. So where did he get it?"

Dr. Muller reappeared, explaining to an anxious Marty close behind: "Take him to your regular dentist in a month, when everything's healed. Then you'll find out if anything else has to be done."

Marty Forster nodded. "I'm not sure where we'll be next month — we try to see our regular dentist if we're back in Vancouver for a bit, but that's not usually till winter. But we'll find someone." He clapped Rick on the shoulder. "We'll be on our way then. Thanks for seeing us after hours. We appreciate it."

Dr. Muller unlocked the door to let them out and stood on the step waving. "I'll see you out at the dig next weekend."

Just then, Marty's cellphone rang.

He waved a hurried goodbye and slapped the phone to his ear.

"Hi, Bill. Where are you? … Here in Dry Valley! … No, we're just leaving the dentist … Rick fell off a bluff … No, he didn't fall as far as you did. He's fine, just looks like a prizefighter."

Tyrannosaurus was a meat eater, so a *T. rex* skull shows a mouthful of long, pointed teeth. They have sharp, wavy edges, like the saw edge on a steak knife. And they're there for the same reason — to help cut tough muscle fibres. Looking at those teeth, it's easy to imagine *Tyrannosaurus* killing its prey with a big chomp, cutting through muscles and armour, and crushing and piercing bones. Some *T. rex* specimens, such as Sue, show matching tooth marks in their own bones, indicating that *T. rex*es used to fight and bite one another as well as their food animals.

Dinosaur teeth are important to paleontologists because they suggest what their owners ate, and how they got it. For example, some predators have many sharp teeth without serrations and were perhaps fish eaters.

Other kinds of dinosaurs have very different kinds of teeth. Giant sauropods have peg- or spoon-shaped teeth, suitable for pulling soft leaves off trees. Hadrosaurian dinosaurs generally had many cheek teeth tightly pressed together to form a ridged "super tooth," good for grinding up lots of coarse vegetation without wearing out.

www.enchantedlearning.com/subjects/dinosaurs/anatomy/Teeth.shtm

Rick rolled his eyes. He walked along the bus, pausing to look at the leaping orca emblem on the side. He ran his finger over the painted mouth of the orca and wondered if its teeth grew as big as the *T. rex* tooth he'd just seen. He shook his muzzy head to clear it. But it was no good. The anaesthetic and painkillers stopped him from thinking clearly. He climbed aboard and fastened his seat belt.

Still talking, Marty got into the driver's seat. "We're just down the road from the coffee shop, Bill. See you in a minute."

Marty stowed the phone, fastened his own seatbelt, and started the engine. "Something's upset Bill Deeley. He wants us to meet him first, before going back to the dig. There's something he wants to tell us. He sounded very mysterious." Marty shrugged. "But that's Bill. Good filmmaker but always dramatizing something." He drove up to Main Street.

The screen door slammed behind them as they entered the hotel coffee shop.

"Hi, Marty," called a voice, and a tall, balding man waved them over to a table by the only open window. He sprawled in his chair, one leg in a cast and propped up on a stool.

Marty strode over, shook his hand, and eyed the leg. "You really did that one in, Bill."

Bill Deeley nodded and pointed to Rick's face with the tip of his cane. "That's pretty spectacular, too."

Rick grinned on one side of his mouth. He and his dad sat down.

A woman's head appeared in the kitchen doorway. Bill

called across to her. "We don't need menus, Tina. Just coffee and ..." he paused and looked at Rick's bruised face "... a chocolate milkshake?"

Rick nodded with enthusiasm.

The woman raised her hand to show she'd heard and soon the smell of fresh coffee permeated the air.

"So, what's the scoop?" asked Marty.

Bill fiddled with his spoon. "It's about the dinosaur dig," he said hesitantly. "First, thanks for taking over for me."

"Hey, you did me a favour," answered Marty. "I had a couple of weeks between projects, so this was a real help. But that's not why you came to see me."

Bill looked serious and dropped his voice. "No, I needed to warn you. Something strange is going on there."

Marty and Rick leaned in closer.

"How strange?" asked Marty.

Bill shrugged. "Odd things, but nothing I can put my finger on ... a weird atmosphere ... a series of small things going wrong ... things being mislaid ... people getting mad at each other for stupid reasons ... and ..." He stopped as Tina brought coffee and the milkshake and placed them on the table.

"Thanks," Marty said.

"Yeah, thankth," spluttered Rick.

"You might as well finish this. No one else will be in today." The woman left the coffee pot in the centre of the table and retreated into the kitchen.

Bill waited until she had vanished.

"Go on?" encouraged Marty.

Bill shifted uncomfortably. "Look, I … I just wanted to warn you in case … since you've got the family with you." His voice tailed off.

"Spit it out, Bill. Give us the straight goods," said Marty.

Bill took a deep breath. "Okay. There is no easy way to say this." He dropped his voice even further. "My accident … I was hanging over the cliff on a rope. It was the best camera angle for the dig …"

"Yes, yes," said Marty, growing impatient. He did things like that all the time.

"I'll swear someone loosened it," Bill said bluntly. He laughed. "Did you choose that T-shirt just for me?"

"It'th ath bad ath you think, and they ARE out to get you," Rick read from the front of Marty's bright red shirt.

Marty laughed. "I didn't know I was going to see you when I put this on. But yes, if you were anyone else, I'd think you were crazy."

Bill thumped the table. "Damn it, Marty, I knew you'd say that." He looked earnestly across at them. "Look, you've got to listen to me. I haven't got any proof, but I honestly think that's what happened." He pointed to his leg. "I persuaded my wife to drive me out here so I could tell you face to face. Now take it seriously."

Marty held his hands up in the air in a gesture of surrender. "Okay, okay. I'm listening. But why would someone want to hurt you?"

Bill sighed. "I can only come up with one reason. Because

I was filming. Maybe I filmed something I wasn't supposed to see. Maybe it wasn't an attempt to hurt me. Maybe the idea was to smash the camera."

Marty frowned. "But the dig's pretty important. The perpetrator must have realized another filmmaker would take over."

Bill nodded. "Sure, but another cameraman wouldn't be familiar with what went on before." He spread his hands in a gesture of resignation. "Oh, I don't know. I've thought and thought about what I might have filmed and who it could possibly be, and no one comes to mind. I just thought I should tell you face to face. It would have sounded even more stupid on the phone."

"Thanks," said Marty. He ran his hand through his hair and a worried frown creased his forehead. "I'll keep my eyes open."

Rick dug his elbow into Marty's arm and desperately struggled to make his words clear. "Dad ... you gotta lithen," he said through lips that felt like balloons. "Victoria thaid the thame thingth."

CHAPTER SEVEN

Marty drove around the potholes, deep in thought.

Rick didn't feel like speaking. His mouth was beginning to throb as the anaesthetic wore off, though he could now move his lips and tongue again.

Marty turned the bus into the farmyard to pick up Willow.

As they came to a stop, Marty finally spoke. "I think both Bill and Victoria are exaggerating events. So don't go spreading rumours." He grinned. "It's bad enough having Victoria shrieking about the curse of the dinosaur's grave."

Rick's lips managed a grin.

"Your mom and I will talk about this and check things out." Marty patted his arm. "You and Willow keep a low profile on the dig. Stay out of everyone's hair. No fooling around and upsetting anyone. Understood?"

Rick nodded. "Okay."

"Hey, they're back!" Victoria, dressed in a brightly coloured Lycra bodysuit, erupted from the barn. Willow followed in a similar outfit that she must have borrowed.

Victoria's shriek brought a large woman to the farmhouse door. Wearing an apron over her jeans, she waved and shouted. "Come on in! Shari's here and we've got supper on the go. I'm Janet Wilkinson, Victoria's mother."

Marty leaped from the bus and went to shake her hand.

Rick approached the girls.

"Hi, Frankenstein." Willow and Victoria went into peals of laughter.

Rick coloured. "I knew one of you would say that," he mumbled.

"Does it still hurt?" Willow advanced a finger toward his cheek. Rick covered his face and stepped back. "Lay off," he warned.

She withdrew her finger and punched his arm sympathetically. "We're working on our dance routine," said Victoria. "Want to come to the barn and watch?"

She and Willow linked arms, and, humming a tune, synchronized some steps.

Rick shook his head. "Could I use your computer? I need to check something on the Net."

"Sure." Victoria turned a pirouette and finished with the splits. "Dad uses it for the farm accounts, but he's at a meeting tonight. We've got unlimited time access on the Net. I'll give you my e-mail address if you want replies to come here."

"Thanks," said Rick, "but I've got my own account."

"We're on holiday," said Willow, doing a pirouette followed by a cartwheel. "Why are you bothering about the Net?"

Rick ignored their gyrations. "I want to see if there's any-where I can buy a *T. rex* tooth. The dentist had one — I guess he must have bought it somewhere."

"You can't buy stuff over the Net," said Willow bossily. "Dad won't let you."

"I'm not going to use his credit card, stupid," argued Rick. "I just want to see if there's any for sale, and how much they are."

It was bedlam in the farmhouse. Victoria's mother, Marty, and Shari were talking up a storm in the kitchen; her older brothers were watching a blaring TV game show; and distant rock music pounded from an upstairs radio. Victoria took Rick into a small office near the stairs. She booted up the computer and showed Rick where to find the Web program, then she and Willow vanished upstairs to try on Victoria's new school clothes. Rick could hear them giggling overhead.

He shut the door and sank back into the chair, enjoying the relative peace. He hit the keys and called up a search engine.

Rick talked to himself as he clicked his way through options. "'Dinosaur Tooth' — naw, too many entries. Let's try '*Tyrannosaurus rex* Tooth.'" After a couple of shots at the correct spelling, Rick found a flood of entries. He waded through them one by one. Suddenly he sat up straight and gave a low whistle. "Wow, wish I was rich," he muttered as he read:

TYRANNOSAURUS REX SKELETON
FOR SALE
Seven million dollars

As the information downloaded, Rick became more and more excited. He took the stairs two at a time and pounded on Victoria's bedroom door. The giggling ceased. "Hey, Willow, Victoria. Come and see this."

The door flew open and there stood Victoria, a hairbrush in her hand, her half-teased hair sticking up all around her face. "What?" she said.

"I've found something amazing on the Net."

The girls looked at each other and shrugged eloquently, but they followed him down and hung over his chair. "This better be good," said Willow.

"It's good, all right. I think I've discovered why the computers were vandalized at the dig. Look at this description of the *T. rex*. I think someone's trying to sell Vicky and doesn't want anyone at the dig to find out."

"No way," argued Victoria. "Impossible."

Willow hung over Rick's shoulder, her eyes eagerly scanning the ad on the screen. "It doesn't say what location the skeleton's from. What makes you think it's Vicky that's for sale, Rick? There must be other *T. rexes* being dug up."

Rick scanned through the site and pointed to the screen. "Read that. What other *T. rex* could it be?"

Willow read out loud.

This *T. rex* has an amazing feature that will revolutionize our knowledge of the species.

"So?" said Victoria.

"Amazing feature. That could be Vicky's ..." Rick looked around guiltily and dropped his voice. "... you know what."

Victoria shook her head decisively. "No way. It really has been kept a secret." She tapped the screen with her fingernail. "Besides, that could refer to anything, like ... like ..."

"Yeah, like what, an ingrown toenail?" said Rick sarcastically.

Willow smothered a chuckle and jabbed him with her elbow.

"... like a skin impression," Victoria finished triumphantly. "There're dinosaurs for sale on the Net sometimes. They tried to sell a *T. rex* that way after Sue was auctioned at Sotheby's. Anyway, Vicky's not for sale. She belongs to the Tyrrell Museum."

"But supposing someone *was* trying to sell her?" Rick persisted.

Victoria laughed. "How could they? They'd have to steal her first. How could you possibly steal a *T. rex*?"

Rick subsided, looking unconvinced.

Victoria started brushing her hair as she walked to the door. "Come on, Willow. I'll show you another new hairstyle."

Willow hesitated.

Rick slumped in his chair, staring at the screen. She lowered her voice so only he could hear. "Rick, were you thinking of the conversation we overheard?"

"Come on, Willow." Victoria turned back, grabbed Willow's sleeve, and tugged her backwards. Willow rolled her eyes at Rick and left the room.

Sue is the most famous *T. rex* of all time, mainly because of the controversies surrounding her.

She (or maybe he) was discovered in South Dakota by — and named after — fossil hunter Sue Hendrickson in 1990. Sue is not only the largest but also the most complete and best-preserved specimen of *T. rex* ever discovered. Her skeleton is more than 12 metres long, and when alive she would have weighed more than six tonnes.

A team led by Peter Larson, a freelance fossil hunter, collected her bones, and she was being prepared for display in Hill City, South Dakota, when the FBI knocked on his door in 1992. Sue was carted away despite protests from Larson and all the children in the town.

For five years, the courts argued about who owned her and decided it was Maurice Williams, who leased the area where she was found. Then she was auctioned in 1997 by Sotheby's, a company better known for fine art than dinosaurs. She was bought for $8.36 million.

Sue is now in the Field Museum in Chicago, where you can visit her. If you don't live nearby, you can go electronically to her Web site.

www.fieldmuseum.org/Sue

Rick kicked the table leg moodily. "Willow might have helped me. We've always worked together on stuff like this." He leaned back in his chair and stared at the ceiling. "Dunno why she's suddenly all interested in dance stuff and clothes and doing her hair when there's a real mystery sitting right under our noses." He sat forward again and glared at the computer screen. "Okay, so I'm on my own. Well, let's see what I can stir up."

He scrolled through the information.

> The specimen is estimated to be about 80% complete. Some parts are still awaiting recovery, and more information on the completeness of the specimen will be posted shortly.

"It does sound as if they're still digging it," Rick muttered. "I bet any money it's Vicky. Now how do I find out more?" He clicked a button and read:

> Potential purchasers should contact us by Friday, August 27th. Only those who have satisfied us of their interest and solvency will be notified of the location where the specimen may be viewed.
> Bids may then be forwarded by e-mail for another week. The successful purchaser will be personally contacted early in September.
>
> Dinosaurs Unlimited

Rick grinned, and his fingers flew as he composed an e-mail. "Better see if I can word this like an uptight business guy," he muttered. "And I'll spell-check this one for sure. Good job my e-mail address doesn't give me away." When it was completed, he read it through.

Dear Dinosaurs Unlimited,

I am a private collector and, like you, have a need for secrecy. I am extremely interested in purchasing a *T. rex*. Money is no object, but for tax reasons I do not want this purchase to be traced through my bank. Once I am convinced that your specimen is genuine and complete, I will make a bid and offer you cash. The handover can be organized at a suitable location for both my agent and yourself.

Sincerely,
Mr. Smith.

Rick sent the message and closed down the computer.

It was late when the Forster-Jennings family finally returned to camp. They had shared a barbecue supper with Victoria's family — all except Rick. Mrs. Wilkinson had made him a bowl of macaroni and cheese.

Shari yawned sleepily. "That was a nice visit, but these early mornings are doing me in. I'm off to bed." She started toward the back of the bus.

"Before you go, Shari, can you give me Bill Deeley's tape?" asked Marty.

Shari looked around. "Sure. Just don't stay up too late watching it." She walked over to the table and opened her briefcase. "Oh. Did you move it, Willow?"

"Sorry, Mom. I wasn't listening. Move what?"

"The videotape I picked up in Calgary. It was in my briefcase."

Willow shook her head.

Shari frowned and scrubbed her fingers through her hair till it stood on end. "I'm sure I didn't put it away." She moved over to the built-in cupboard that housed the video unit and screen, opened the door, and checked through the shelved tapes. "It's not here." Her voice had a distinct note of panic.

Marty walked over and patted her shoulder. "Calm down. It can't be far. We'll find it. Come on kids. Help search the bus."

There was no sign of the missing tape.

Everyone sat down around the table. Shari's eyes were large and dark in her white face. "I can't believe I've lost it. I've never lost a tape."

"Come on, Dad. Tell her she hasn't lost it," burst out Rick.

"What do you mean?" Shari looked from Rick to Marty.

Marty put his arm around her shoulders and gave her a squeeze. "Rick's right. This is a crazy idea, but you might not have lost it. Was your briefcase on the table when we were filming at the dig?"

66

Shari nodded. "Yes. I dropped it there when we got to camp."

"Then the tape might have been stolen," Marty said seriously.

Willow looked startled. "So my ditzy dance mate Victoria was right. The curse of the dinosaur's grave is really happening!"

CHAPTER EIGHT

"No arguing. Off to bed. Your mom and I need to talk." Marty pointed toward the bedrooms.

Despite their protests, Willow and Rick were banished.

Willow followed Rick to his room and perched on the end of his bunk bed. "So what do you think is going on?" she whispered.

"Why should you care?" asked Rick. "You're too busy with Victoria."

"No, I'm not." Willow was stung to the quick. "I want to help. I just don't often get the chance to dance. It doesn't mean I'm not interested in the dinosaur's curse."

"You've got a funny way of showing it." Rick drew up his knees and sat hunched up on his pillow. "I tried to show you what I thought was happening at Victoria's ... and you took off."

"I'm sorry, Rick. It's just ... I don't have many friends. We move around too much to hang out with other kids as much as I'd like."

"It's the same problem for me," Rick muttered. "I just get to know somebody and we're off to the next province."

Willow gazed helplessly at her younger brother. "I know … but you seemed to be all involved in the dinosaur dig. You weren't interested in what Victoria and I'd been doing."

Rick sighed. "It's great on the dig, but something weird is going on and I need help to sort it out. I thought you'd help me. We've always solved mysteries together before."

"Okay, okay. I'm here now. Tell me the latest."

Rick filled her in about meeting Bill Deeley.

"Wow! So Bill told Dad it was no accident, then you came home and found the tape was missing! No wonder Mom and Dad freaked."

Rick nodded. "I put that story together with all the stuff Victoria told me. I hadn't believed her at first. I thought she was a flake. But now I think everything *is* linked. Someone is trying to sell Vicky."

"Okay. How do you work that out?" Willow leaned against the wall and tucked her toes under the comforter. She fixed her eyes on her brother.

Rick sat up straighter. It wasn't often his older sister asked his opinion. "It started before we came. Some small bones went missing."

"Why would anyone want to steal small bones? I'd want a big one."

"Because the person who wanted to sell Vicky — let's call him X — "

"What if it's a her?" Willow said with a smirk.

"Whatever," muttered Rick. "Anyway, X needed to show proof to someone, so they took the small bones."

Willow nodded. "Okay. That would fit. What happened next?"

"The map disappeared."

Willow looked puzzled. "So, get a new map!"

Rick chuckled. "I said that! But this map's special. Doug drew it to show how the bones lie in the quarry. Then it turned up two days later in the kitchen trailer where no one would have left it. Now what if it was taken to be photocopied as more proof?"

"So then it could be returned? You're brilliant, Rick. What else did you work out?"

"Well, one day Doug's truck didn't work. Then it was fine the next day. I checked. It didn't work on the day the map was missing."

"I don't get the connection," said Willow.

"Neither did anyone else. They were just frustrated," replied Rick. "But suppose X was scared he might be seen photocopying the map. Suppose X fixed the truck so nobody could go into town."

"Oh boy, you've really figured it out." Willow clasped her knees and rocked to and fro with excitement. "Now the big one. If Bill Deeley's right, X was scared Bill had filmed something that might give him away."

"Yes, but I haven't figured out what yet," Rick admitted.

Willow chewed her lip thoughtfully. "Maybe ... X was caught doing something weird, like being in the quarry at the wrong time ... when something went missing?"

"That would work," agreed Rick. "But why would he organize

an accident if the evidence was already on the tape?"

"To get a chance to steal the tape?"

"Or to get Bill off the dig so the coast was clear in the future?"

"But we turned up with the tape, so X snitched it from Mom's briefcase," finished Willow triumphantly.

"Don't forget the computer meltdown," Rick grinned. "If I was selling a dinosaur over the Net, I sure wouldn't want the dig people to find out."

"So you think X fixed Doug's computer. Wow. It all fits."

Despite his beat-up face, Rick managed to look complacent. "Told you so. But it only made sense this afternoon when I found the *T. rex* for sale. I'm sure it's Vicky."

"It can't be Vicky," said Willow. "*How* could someone steal her? She's enormous."

Rick shrugged. "Haven't got a clue. Gonna help me?"

"You bet. Are we going to tell Mom and Dad what you've figured out?"

Rick snorted. "Are you kidding? They wouldn't believe me. And if they did, they wouldn't let us stay if they thought it was dangerous. I might have already blown it by telling Dad that Victoria agreed with Bill. That's why he took the missing tape so seriously."

"Mom's pretty upset about the tape. She might make us leave anyway," groaned Willow.

Rick stifled a yawn and rubbed his eyes. "I can't think any more. I gotta sleep. The doctor gave me some painkillers that make me dopey."

This list shows the most famous examples of *T. rex* in order of discovery.

1. The first specimen, excavated by Barnum Brown in Montana in 1902, was named *Tyrannosaurus rex* by Henry Fairfield Osborn in 1905. Fifty percent complete, it is now in the Carnegie Museum of Natural History in Pittsburgh.

2. Black Beauty was found in 1981 by three students in Alberta. Twenty-five percent complete, it was mounted at the Royal Tyrrell Museum and also travelled with a touring exhibit.

3. Stan was discovered in 1987 in South Dakota and collected by the Black Hills Institute. It is 60–65 percent complete.

4. The first 80 percent complete specimen was discovered by Kathy Wankel in Montana in 1988 and excavated by John Horner in 1990.

5. Sue was found by Sue Hendrickson in South Dakota in 1990. Estimated at 90–95 percent complete.

6. Z-rex, found in 1992 in South Dakota, was offered at auction for $12 million.

7. Scotty, found in 1994 in Saskatchewan, is now being displayed in its own interpretive centre near Eastend.

www.dinocountry.com/
www.dinosauria.com/jdp/trex/specimens.html

Willow slid off the bed. "All right. We'll deal with Mom and Dad tomorrow. I'll try and think up a good reason why we should stay."

She crept back to her bedroom.

After supper, Jimmy was working on his own behind the neck vertebrae when Wally came stumbling along the path in the twilight.

"No, there's still no skull," Jimmy said, as Wally peered into the shadowy excavation.

"Might not matter anyhow," said Wally. "Little brother says the big man's getting cold feet."

"What! He can't do that!"

Wally laughed. "Whatcha gonna do? How do you sue a multi-millionaire over a shady deal with no contract to back you up?"

"Well, we'll just have to find someone else. You go back and tell your brother that we'll have to advertise …" Jimmy began to chew his fingernails.

"We already fixed it," Wally growled. "He's putting the word out to the right people. And he set up a Web site yesterday. It might pick up a few more possibles."

"He did *what*!" yelped Jimmy. "What if someone traces it?"

"Strictly anonymous," said Wally calmly. "We gotta take the risk. We're in this too deep to back out now. And we've laid out too much cash."

Willow and Rick woke early. They warily entered the living

area wondering what their parents were going to say.

Shari and Marty were drinking coffee. They were not talking and looked serious. Shari gave them a tired smile. "Hi, kids."

Marty fetched a jug of juice from the fridge. "Ready for breakfast?"

The kids nodded.

Willow decided to take the bull by the horns. "You still worried about the tape, Mom?"

"Yes," said Shari. "Your Dad and I have decided …"

Thump. Thump. The bus shook gently as someone knocked on the side. Shari broke off and turned toward the door.

A figure mounted the steps and waved through the steamy window.

Marty got up and opened the door.

Heather's round face came into view, smiling cheerfully. "Good morning, everyone. I'm glad you're awake. I was afraid I might be too early." She handed a videotape box to Shari. "I thought you might be worried about this. I found it on the ground last night. I figured you must have dropped it."

Shari gasped. She opened the box. There was the missing tape. "Thank you, thank you, Heather. I missed it when we got back late last night. You have no idea how worried I've been."

Willow chuckled. "So you dropped it after all, Mom. Great. That's solved that. Now can Rick and I go off to the dig to join the crew?"

CHAPTER NINE

Willow and Rick jogged along the badland trail. The early morning was still cool, but a hazy blue sky warned of heat to come.

Willow was still chuckling. "Boy, we all got wound up for nothing last night. Thank goodness Heather found the tape."

"*If* she found it," Rick muttered.

"Oh, come on. I thought you liked Heather. You don't think she stole it, do you?"

"I dunno." Rick flushed. "I like her. It's just that … well … suppose Heather is X. She could have got the tape and checked it last night before giving it back. There's a video player in the crew tent."

"I see what you mean." Willow thought for a minute. "Victoria said Heather looked guilty yesterday afternoon. What if she slipped back to camp and stole the tape then? No one would have noticed."

Rick kicked a loose rock in frustration. "I don't want Heather to be X."

"Neither do I," admitted Willow. "I'd rather it was Jimmy."

"Me too, but we've got nothing to go on."

"Anyway, X doesn't have to be on the dig. The camp's wide open. Other people could sneak in and steal stuff."

They reached the heap of shale where Rick had slipped down the slope and injured himself.

"Did you bring your finds?" asked Willow.

"In my pocket," said Rick, feeling their hard shapes with his hand. "If Doug's on site, I can show them to him."

"There he is," said Willow, turning the corner.

"Good," said Rick. "Here goes."

He pulled the pieces of fossil out of his pocket and ran over to Doug.

"I found these yesterday." Rick held them out. "Is it all right if I keep them?"

"Were they loose on the surface?" Doug asked as he glanced at the fragments. He put on his glasses and looked closer, peering at all the surfaces, and gently put two pieces together.

"Are they pieces of tooth?" asked Rick eagerly.

"Sure. Where did you find them?" Doug smiled at Rick's enthusiasm.

"Back around the corner, in the canyon. There's a big piece too, but it's still stuck in the rock."

Doug looked excited. "Why don't you show me?"

"It's up here. Where I fell."

"This could be important," Doug said. "We're on the other side of the bluff from the excavation."

"Think they might be Vicky's teeth?" said Rick eagerly.

Doug held up his hand with his fingers crossed. Rick and Willow laughed. They all surveyed the steep badland slope.

"The fragments were scattered on the canyon floor, so I checked further up the slope to see where they came from," explained Rick.

"Good. That's what I would do," said Doug.

"The bits of teeth were scattered halfway up. The big piece is in the rock just … there …" Rick tailed off as he realized he couldn't see it. "I'm sure it was there," he said, puzzled.

Doug turned his eyes from the slope to Rick's face. "It's easy to lose the spot unless you've marked the place. The badlands all look the same."

"No, it was here," Rick insisted. He pointed to the fresh rock lying on the ground. "That's where I landed." He scrambled up the ragged scar. "There's chisel marks in the rock. Someone's pried it out."

Doug climbed up beside him.

"You're right." He looked suspiciously at Rick. "You're sure you or your sister didn't take it?"

Rick slid down to the ground. "Why would I show you the place if I'd taken it?" He stalked away, his back stiff with indignation.

"I'm sorry." Doug jumped down and caught up with him. "I had to ask. But there's nothing to see now. Got to get back to the dig. I've got too much to do there."

Rick said nothing, his eyes watering with anger and disappointment.

Willow stared thoughtfully up at the rock face.

Rick wandered restlessly around the dig, too upset to settle. He passed Jimmy and Wally, still excavating into the hillside, then finally hunkered down to watch Luisa. Her usual black shirt and jeans were heavily stained with white drips as she dipped a strip of burlap in a bucket of white goo, then carefully draped the wet plaster bandage over the femur.

"Are there dinosaurs in Spain?" asked Rick.

"Some," said Luisa, smiling. "And lots of *rastrillada* — trackways of dinosaurs. I have been casting the tracks, but I did not have the experience digging up bones like these." She paused and gazed into the distance. "It is like this in Spain in the summer — sunny and hot." She made a little grimace. "And though I am enjoying being here, I am missing my friends. *Habla español?* Do you speak any Spanish?"

"Me! No. Though I had a friend from Mexico in Vancouver. *Hola* is hello, right?"

Luisa laughed. "That's right." She began to work again. "Now we are finding new bones in Spain, and I needed to get new experience. So I came to study at the Tyrrell. Now I know how to plaster big bones, and I can direct a dig when I get home."

"It's like the cast I had on my broken arm," Rick commented, watching as her long fingers pressed the soft bandage into every recess.

"That's exactly what it is. Once it's hardened, it holds the bone rigid, so it won't break when we lift it."

"How are you going to lift it?" asked Rick curiously. "It's gigantic."

In the early days, finding dinosaurs was easier than getting them home safely. When geologist Joe Tyrrell took an *Albertosaurus* skull out of the Red Deer River badlands in 1884, he packed the bones in straw and drove his wagon slowly and carefully to the nearest railway at Calgary. His specimen got to Ottawa intact.

Later collectors made rafts and floated down the deep canyon of the Red Deer River. Thomas Weston was the first to explore this way, but he didn't know how to protect the bones, so his finds were shaken to pieces later when they were carried in wagons over rough trails.

American collectors developed the technique of plastering bones, and Barnum Brown from New York brought the technique to Canada when he began a five-year voyage down the river in 1910. The Geological Survey of Canada hired veteran collector Charles Hazelius Sternberg with his three sons to compete with Brown in what has become known as the Canadian Dinosaur Rush. They too worked from a raft and plastered bones. Both teams unloaded their finds when the river reached a bridge or ferry. Railcar loads of bones were sent off to museums in Ottawa and New York each year.

By the 1920s, small cars and trucks carried out fossil bones over muddy roads. Today, the big plastered blocks are lifted by crane or helicopter. They are loaded onto a truck and driven carefully to the museum over paved highways.

"By helicopter," Luisa replied.

Rick's eyes widened. "Far out!"

"Not all the way to the museum," Luisa explained, laughing as his eyes wandered across the sky. "It'll lift the bones to the top of the cliff and load them onto a truck."

Shari tapped Rick on the shoulder. "Rick. I need to talk to you for a minute."

They walked out of earshot of the workers. "What's the scoop on the teeth?" she asked. "Doug said you reported finding some, but they weren't there."

Rick's stomach tied itself in knots again. "It's true," he said. "It was one tooth, and someone's taken it."

"But it wasn't you?"

"No way. I'm the one who discovered it," Rick said, still angry. "I would have taken it if it was loose, but it wasn't," he finished honestly.

"Doug needed to ask because you'd told everyone you wanted your own dinosaur tooth," Shari explained. She looked over at the crew. "I wonder who else could have taken it?"

Rick shrugged. "How do I know? I was at the doctor and the dentist the rest of the afternoon." He looked up at his mother. "I couldn't have taken it without someone seeing. Heather was there while I was sleeping, then Willow and Victoria were with me, but they weren't interested in climbing up the badlands. The only person I told about the tooth was Dr. Muller. He collects teeth. He showed me one in his office. What about him?"

Shari sighed. "Guess we'll never know without proof. It's one more silly mystery." She gave Rick a quick hug. "We believe you. Don't worry about it any more." She looked up and realized that Heather was standing within earshot. Their eyes met briefly. Heather flushed and moved away.

"Doug, Rick … come and see!" Willow ran out of the canyon shouting and gestured them to follow her. "Look at this," she panted. "I used a pick. Rick was right about the teeth. There's more in the rock. And some bone."

Doug raced into the canyon. Rick scampered behind.

Willow had climbed up and chipped away the surface rock where Rick's tooth had vanished. She had uncovered the tops of three teeth, attached to a ridge of bone. Their smooth surfaces contrasted with the rough sandstone around them.

"You're right, Willow," said Doug, trying to stay calm. "And it doesn't look as if you've done any damage — but let me do it next time."

He probed gently, prying more rock off the surface of the bone. "That could be the upper jaw of a *T. rex*. Thanks to you two, it looks as though Vicky might not have lost her head, after all."

His studied professionalism collapsed. Doug gave a cheer, grabbed Willow and Rick, and whirled them in a dance down the length of the canyon.

A grinning Marty captured it on film.

CHAPTER TEN

"This should be our job," said Wally.

For the first time, there was open disagreement among the crew.

Jimmy and Wally stood on a ledge they had chopped out below the skull, blocking the way, with tools at the ready.

"Sorry," Doug said, shaking his head. "We're short of time. The chopper's coming in two days. All the volunteers are on the plastering, and you two are the only ones with the experience to drill into that cliff after the neck. It's obviously broken, otherwise the skull wouldn't be so far away. You need to drill out more rock in the quarry and find that last vertebrae."

Wally made a growl of protest.

Doug ignored it. "You know a skull is rare, one of the most important parts of the skeleton. The shale here is unstable. It needs *my* experience to get it out without damage. Rick and Willow found it, and are light enough to climb up and work above me, so it makes sense for them to help."

Wally and Jimmy glared at everyone and stomped off round the bluff, muttering.

Rick and Willow surreptitiously gave each other the thumbs-up.

Doug gestured toward the badlands slope. "It's a tricky spot. I can stand on the ledge to reach the teeth and upper jaw. But I can't reach on top. And you see how above the skull there is just a narrow crumbly ridge, so it isn't safe for me to climb down on to it from the cliff. I could hang on to a rope, but I'd damage the skull or keep falling off. If you weren't here, we'd have to spend a week putting up scaffolding so we could work safely. But if one of you will climb up, I could support you while you scrape away the loose upper surface."

"What will the other person do?" asked Willow.

Doug laughed. "Shift the rubble as it falls to our feet. You can take it in turns. Now watch my technique." Lightly using the hammer and chisel, Doug tapped around the front of the skull, expertly flaking off small chips of rock.

Marty's camera zoomed in as, slowly and surely, Vicky's head emerged.

It was slow, tiring work. Willow and Rick took turns shifting rubble without complaint. The exciting bit was clearing the rock on top of the skull.

"I feel like a real paleontologist," announced Rick as he carefully chipped away above the eye socket.

"I feel like a weightlifter," grumbled Doug, supporting Rick's feet in tenuous toeholds.

"And I feel like a garbage collector," added Willow,

returning with an empty wheelbarrow from the discard pile.

Marty grinned. Good, they'd forgotten he was there. He recorded it all.

The morning wore on. The sun blazed down unrelentingly onto their ledge, but Doug, Willow, and Rick were oblivious.

"What a lot of teeth. Now Vicky's grinning." Willow grinned too as Doug exposed tooth number twelve. "It's like she's got a secret, and she's not going to tell."

"I wish she'd tell us what happened to her lower jaw," grumbled Doug. "It's definitely missing. How frustrating!"

"The rock below the teeth is real loose." Willow was on her knees scraping away by Doug's feet. "It keeps sliding and covering the ledge. Shall we clear it?"

"Why not." Doug leaped down. "I'll check on the plastering back in the quarry so you've got room to work."

Rick abandoned the wheelbarrow and climbed up to help Willow. They dug and scraped with trowels to clear the ledge below the skull, but as fast as they worked, more shale showered down.

"What's all this white stuff?" Rick held out his trowel.

"Beats me," said Willow. "I've found some too."

They tipped the material on their trowels into the wheelbarrow and continued.

"Here's a square of old burlap. Where did that come from?" Willow held it up, looking puzzled. She put it on one side to show Doug.

Rick scraped his trowel along the ledge and pushed a pile of shale over into the wheelbarrow. As it dropped, something glinted.

Rick leaned over and picked it out. He started to laugh. "I thought Vicky was supposed to be a meat eater."

"What do you mean?" asked Willow, brushing a strand of sweat-dampened hair out of her eyes and tucking it back under her head scarf.

"She's been eating sardines," Rick said with a chuckle, holding up an empty sardine can.

Willow looked from the can to the rock they were clearing. "Why would someone have a picnic here? The can wasn't on the surface, it was buried under all this stuff!"

A distant rumble of thunder made her statement more dramatic.

"Let's see what else we can find." Rick started sifting through the loose rubble again.

By the time Doug returned, they'd found more white bits to add to the burlap sacking and sardine can and were laughing hysterically at a fragment of old yellowed newspaper.

"This is insane. Vicky reads, too," said Willow. She thrust the piece of paper at Doug. "Go on. Explain that."

"You kids are certainly on a roll," said Doug with obvious admiration. "You just might have solved the mystery of the missing lower jaw."

"Really?" Rick and Willow chorused.

Doug poked through the strange pile. "These white flecks are plaster. That and the burlap sacking tell me an

85

earlier paleontologist has been working here."

"You're kidding," Rick said in a disgusted tone. "You mean we're not the first to find Vicky?"

Doug grinned. "Not quite. We're the first to find the skeleton, and you're the first to find the skull; otherwise they'd have been taken out long ago. But this old junk …" he waved the scrap of newspaper "… tells me someone else probably found the lower jaw. It must have separated and eroded out first." He let a handful of rubble trickle through his fingers. "People have been finding dinosaurs in the badlands for over a century. This is debris from an earlier excavation." Doug waved the newspaper excitedly. "We may be able to date the dig." He scanned the paper. "This is a Depression story, so that makes it during the 1930s. But who was the collector? Now there's a nice little mystery."

Rick pretended to open the can. "Someone who was hungry and loved sardines." He fumbled and dropped it.

Willow picked it up. "Look, the key is sticking out of the wrong side. You wouldn't open it that way. It was somebody who was left-handed."

"Terrific!" said Doug with enthusiasm. "We're looking for a left-handed dinosaur collector who worked here in the thirties. You've got the sort of inquiring minds that make good paleontologists." He rose and pulled a plastic bag out of his pocket. He dropped in the newspaper. Willow added the sardine can and Rick the burlap. "Unfortunately, I was coming to tell you to pack up."

"Why? This is really exciting," protested Willow.

"A thunderstorm's rolling in. We've tarped the plaster blocks so they won't get wet, but let's get back to camp before it pours." Doug glanced at Marty. "Do you guys need plastic to keep the cameras dry?"

"Thanks, we've got bags," said Marty, as the first heavy drops came down. "Come on, kids. Boot it. You can help again later."

>>>>>>>>>>>>>> **Finding old quarries** <<<<<<<<<<

Pioneer dinosaur collectors took only the best and easiest specimens and often didn't have time to look for all the pieces. Modern paleontologists still search for missing bits from important specimens.

But the early quarries aren't always easy to find. Modern dinosaur experts use old field notes and photographs to identify sites of former excavations. Retired expert Charles M. Sternberg helped by identifying many of the quarries he remembered working on in Dinosaur Provincial Park in Alberta.

Sometimes valuable finds are recovered from forgotten sites. A partial *T. rex* skeleton found by Sternberg in 1946 was left in the rock because he didn't have the tools to work in the very hard sandstone. Tyrrell Museum staff rediscovered it after he died, and the specimen was excavated half a century later.

CHAPTER ELEVEN

The rain poured down in torrents for more than an hour. The dry badlands thirstily soaked it up. Eventually a fine drizzle set in. Thoroughly bored after the excitement of the morning, Rick and Willow sloshed through the wet ground to the kitchen trailer in search of hot chocolate.

Charlie was placing two lunches on the counter.

Wally entered, followed by Jimmy. They walked over to the counter.

"These ours?" Jimmy grunted.

Charlie nodded.

"Are you leaving camp?" asked Willow.

"Yup," replied Wally. "Going to take the SUV up the hill. Brrooom."

"Why, have we finished for the day?" said Rick, puzzled. "It's only just lunchtime."

Jimmy gestured through the open door. "It's wet."

"It's drizzle," objected Rick. "I don't mind being out in it."

Jimmy and Wally exchanged glances.

"Might be a little slippy," said Jimmy.

"It won't worry me," said Rick, raring to go.

Wally and Jimmy eyed each other.

Wally pointed to the nearest bluff. "I'll race you to the top."

"When?" said Rick.

"Now," Wally replied with a grin. He stepped outside the trailer. "Come on."

"Don't do it, Rick," Willow said quietly. "Mom and Dad will be furious if you mash your face again."

Rick ignored her. He and Wally squared off.

Jimmy and Willow watched from the doorway.

Jimmy counted down: "One, two, three, GO!"

Rick flung himself in a great leap up the slope, only to find the rocks now seemed to be covered by a couple of centimetres of slippery wet goo. He slid gracefully back down to the bottom on his belly, his hands scrabbling through the slime unable to catch hold of anything.

Covered in mud, Rick turned to see that Wally hadn't even started. He and Jimmy were leaning against the trailer doorway roaring with laughter.

"Sorry," said Wally through his guffaws. "I forgot to explain. No one works in the rain. It makes the clay too soft and slippery."

Rick glared at them and stomped back to the big blue bus.

Willow pushed past Jimmy and Wally. "Creeps," she muttered. "Bet they're still mad because we found the skull."

She ran after Rick and caught him at the steps of the bus.

"I wish those idiots would do something else suspicious

instead of Heather," she said. "I hate them. It's people like them who steal things. Not her."

Rick nodded glumly and headed for the shower.

The drizzle stopped. Suddenly the sun came out and the ground steamed. Since the dig was on hold, Rick and Willow sat on the bus steps, eating cherries and competing at spitting pits.

A mud-spattered four-wheel drive entered the camp and honked. Victoria waved madly from the passenger seat. "Hey, you two. Want to come to the farm? See if Rick has e-mail?"

"Okay!" said Rick. "I'll ask Mom and Dad. They're napping."

"Where were you this morning?" asked Willow. She offered cherries to Victoria and Eddie, her older brother.

"Shopping in Drumheller." Victoria pulled a face. "Only school supplies though. No new clothes."

"You missed out on a great find." Willow grinned wickedly. "Doug's renaming your dinosaur."

"What?" Victoria's jaw dropped. "What's it going to be called?"

"Ricky," Willow said with a poker face. "Rick and I found the skull."

Victoria gulped, swallowed a whole cherry, and had a coughing fit.

Willow looked guilty and thumped her on the back. "It's okay. I'm only teasing. Well ... I'm teasing about the name. But we did find the skull."

"You bag!" Victoria wiped her streaming eyes and blew her nose. "I really believed you."

Willow laughed. "You should have seen your face."

"We can go." Rick ran over. "Dad's turned on his cell-phone. He wants us to call him for a pickup."

"I'll bring you back," Eddie offered. "You need a four-wheel drive to get in and out of the coulee. Your bus will never make it till the road's dry."

"I'll tell them." Rick stuck his head inside the bus. "Eddie's going to bring us back!" he hollered. He ran back to the car. "Let's boogie."

Wally and Jimmy were burning down the wet highway, throwing up spray from the glistening black pavement. Jimmy was driving, and Wally leaned back with the hat over his eyes, crooning a country song.

"Hey, Wally," Jimmy interrupted. "We're getting close. You know this country better than I do."

Wally tipped back his hat, sat up, and surveyed the landscape. "Milk River Ridge over that side," he gestured vaguely. "Not many roads over there." He gazed over at Jimmy's side. "See that hill? That's the nearest of the Three Buttes. The Sweetgrass Hills. There's a good road north of the border in that direction. That's our best bet. Ranch country both sides of the Medicine Line. Got a lead on a backcountry trail from my bro."

"Let's check it out," said Jimmy quietly, slowing as the green road sign came into view.

The three kids gathered around the computer.

"Sweet. The dinosaur site has sent a reply." Shaking with excitement, Rick opened it.

> **Dear Mr. Smith,**
>
> **Thank you for your interest. While we appreciate your wish for anonymity, if you are still an interested purchaser we will need proof of your ability to pay the asking price. Please send us references and more personal information. You may be interested to know we have now verified the skeleton includes the skull.**
>
> **Dinosaurs Unlimited**

Willow gave a whoop. "Rick! They've heard about the skull. It *is* Vicky they're trying to sell."

Rick gazed dolefully at the screen. "I know, I know," he muttered. "But how do I prove I'm a millionaire? Who'd have that much to spend?"

"The president of an oil company?" suggested Victoria.

"A Dutch banker," Willow suggested at the same time. She laughed. "Could be one and the same. Make him own other stuff too."

"Like what?" said Rick.

"Well, he could also own a bank and have fancy real estate, say in the West Indies."

"How come you know this stuff?" asked Victoria.

"I had to follow the daily news on the Net last year as part of my home schooling." She turned to Rick. "Move over."

Rick slid off the chair and Willow sat down. Her fingers danced over the keys.

"We just borrow names of a European bank, an oil company and some small island in the West Indies. If X is stealing a dinosaur, she's not going to blow her identity by checking references."

"Here we are. Write this down. Your name is Wilhelm Van Bosch … you're a major shareholder in the Luxembourg Premier Bank, run Venezuelan Oil Corporation, and own an island off Trinidad. There! You, little brother, are now a billionaire!"

"Should we tell anyone what we've found on the Net?" asked Victoria, as they closed down the computer.

"We think it's Vicky," said Willow practically, "but how can we prove it? And we've already tried all the other evidence on Doug. He'd just laugh at us."

"Maybe X is Doug," said Victoria mysteriously. "He'd be in the best position to steal the dinosaur when it's all collected. Perhaps we shouldn't tell him anything or we'll all be in terrible danger."

Rick and Willow guffawed.

"Seriously," said Rick, "if we convince our parents something's really going on, they won't let us stay on the dig. And it's too much fun to miss."

"Besides," added Willow, "we may be wrong about it

Black market fossils

In 1993, a stegosaur from the United States was sold to a Japanese museum over the protests of many Americans. While this transfer was legal, many more fossils cross borders without publicity and sometimes without permission.

Smuggling and the secret sale of cigarettes, liquor, and drugs — the "black market" — is often in the news, but we don't hear much about the illegal trade in fossils. Scientifically important specimens are smuggled out of the countries where they are found and sold openly at rock and fossil shows, or secretly by private arrangement, sometimes over the Internet.

Public museums no longer support illegal trading. But some unethical private collectors still fund thefts and smuggling, satisfied to decorate their boardrooms or homes with a spectacular, but illegal, specimen.

http://news.nationalgeographic.com/news/
2001/08/0823_wiredinohunters.html

being Vicky. If we tell anyone, they'll never let us forget how stupid we've been. As it is, if it's really another *T. rex*, we're just having fun and no harm's been done."

"Yeah," said Rick. "Watch and wait."

94

CHAPTER TWELVE

It was Thursday — helicopter day — and the weather was perfect. The sun blazed down, and only a faint breeze stirred the scrubby grass on top of the cliff. In the quarry below, the crew laboured in stifling heat.

For two days nothing suspicious had happened. Everyone was far too busy working.

It was Willow's turn to watch for the truck from the top of the cliff. She pulled off her head scarf and shook out her fair hair. The breeze lifted the strands and cooled her neck.

A distant movement across the fields caught her eye. She leaped to her feet, stuffing the head scarf in her pocket. "Here comes the truck!" she yelled.

The dig crew redoubled their efforts at organizing the site for the helicopter lift.

Marty was checking his camera and spare cassettes.

Willow cut across the pasture to meet the truck. She jumped up and down, waving, and caught the driver's attention. He smiled and gave a wave of acknowledgment. The gigantic flatbed towed by a tractor unit moved cautiously off the dirt road into the field, slowed, and stopped.

The driver rolled down his window. "Is the ground hard all the way in?" he called to Willow over the noisy motor.

"Yes," she gasped, a bit out of breath. "My name's Willow. Doug said I should show you where to go."

"Okay," he said. "Hop in."

"Really?" She ran round to the other side and clambered up the cab steps, eagerly slipped into the comfortable passenger seat, and gazed around. "I'm Al," said the driver, smiling at Willow's enthusiasm.

The cab was roomy, and a small forest of levers stuck up between her and the driver. He shifted into gear and eased the truck slowly forward while Willow continued to inspect her surroundings. Through a doorway between the seats, she could see a bunch of cupboards and even a bed behind a half-pulled curtain. "Hey, it's like a gypsy caravan," she said. "You can live in here."

"Yeah," said Al. "The bed's for long trips, so one driver can sleep while the other drives. But this gypsy doesn't have a crystal ball — which way do I turn here?"

"Sorry," said Willow. "You need to go toward the cliff edge first. Doug said you could nose in that way," she pointed, "then back up to the top of the cliff."

As she spoke, Doug's head appeared over the edge of the cliff. He waved as he saw them, clambered up, and guided the truck into place. Al and Willow clambered out of the cab and jumped down to the prairie.

"Is everything ready?" Al asked.

Doug proudly surveyed the scatter of white plaster bundles below. He checked everything. There was the pelvis, sections of legs, backbones and ribs, the forearm, and the small but priceless parcel containing the young *T. rex*.

"Everything's plastered," he said with satisfaction. "Even Willow's skull on the other side of the bluff. Each cast is marked, and the lifting ropes and loops are in place."

"But Wally and Jimmy are still drilling," said Willow.

"I've told them they could lay off, but they're incredibly keen. They figure if they deepen that trench, they'll find the elusive missing vertebra." He pointed to the narrow ridge leading to the bluff. "It's probably below there, somewhere between the skeleton and your skull over the other side."

"But even if they find it, they can't plaster it before the helicopter comes," said Willow, a worried frown furrowing her forehead.

"No, but we could haul one vertebra out manually." Doug gave a sigh of pleasure. "Looks like Vicky could be the most complete *T. rex* ever found. She's worn well for sixty-eight million years. Thanks for keeping watch, Willow. You're off duty now."

As Doug turned to chat with Al, Willow waved, then clambered down the rope at Deeley's Dive. She landed safely on the dig site and patted the biggest plaster parcel as she passed.

"Vicky, this has been your home for a long time," she whispered. "But soon you'll have a new one in the museum."

She ran to the canyon to find Rick.

The skull was now sitting in the middle of the trail, a white package as long as Rick was tall. After it had been exposed and plastered on one side, it had been carefully winched down from its perch on the ridge. Once on the ground, it had been turned over, the other side had been cleared of surplus rock, and the plaster jacket completed. Now Luisa was fixing ropes to the metal rods which added extra strength to the plaster-encased skull.

"Where's Rick?" Willow asked.

Luisa looked around vaguely. "He was here. I think he went back down the trail toward camp."

Willow headed down the trail after him.

"Psst." Rick's head popped out from behind a rock. "Over here."

"What are you doing?"

"Shhh. I'm setting a trap."

"Who for?" asked Willow.

"Dr. Muller, in case he's X. Luisa told me he's on his way. I've put a piece of *T. rex* tooth in the middle of the path. Now shut up and watch."

Willow and Rick crouched behind the boulder.

Dr. Muller walked along, whistling cheerfully. He saw the tooth fragment, bent down, and picked it up. He frowned, looked around, then slipped it in his pocket, and walked on.

"See that!" whispered Rick. "He's taken it. I bet he stole my other find."

"Watch what he does with it," cautioned Willow.

Keeping well behind, they followed Dr. Muller to the dig.

"Hello there!" Dr. Muller shouted as he climbed up to the quarry.

"No toothaches in Dry Valley today?" Doug called down from the bluff, where he was talking with the driver beside the parked truck.

"I put a notice on the door telling everyone to come back tomorrow," Dr. Muller laughed. "I couldn't miss this."

Doug rapidly descended the rope.

"I've got something to show you." Dr. Muller pulled the tooth fragment out of his pocket. "Does this look familiar?"

Rick grunted as Willow dug him in the ribs.

Doug turned the fragment over. "It's a piece of broken tooth — but you know that."

The dentist laughed.

"It looks like one of the pieces Rick found. The ones that led him and Willow to the skull. I said he could keep them for now. They didn't seem to fit any of the teeth left in Vicky's skull."

They both turned as Rick and Willow scrambled up to the dig.

"This yours, Rick?" Doug held it out.

Rick's cheeks were scarlet. "I must have dropped it," he mumbled. "Thanks."

"Who was caught in your trap?" whispered Willow.

Rick stuck out his tongue.

Back in the camp, Shari was excitedly checking her camera and strapping on a safety harness. She was going to film from the open door of the helicopter. She'd done it before, but always nervously looked over her equipment several times.

Shari jotted a few short notes in her notebook, then spotted Heather sitting by herself with a cup of coffee at the picnic tables.

Shari gazed at her thoughtfully and walked over. "Ready for the celebratory dinner in town this evening?"

Heather stirred her coffee but didn't meet Shari's eye. "I suppose." She sighed. "I leave for England on Sunday."

Shari chose her words with care. "Rick tells me you have a grandson his age."

Heather's eyes filled with tears. "Yes, Paul. Rick reminds me of him. They're both so keen on dinosaurs."

"But you don't see much of Paul?" said Shari sympathetically.

Heather blew her nose hard. "My daughter and I don't get on very well."

Shari spoke slowly. "So when you saw what excited Rick, you thought Paul would be excited about the same things ... like teeth?"

Heather turned white. Her mouth made a little "oh" of surprise.

"Rick was so disappointed when the one he found went missing." Shari waited.

Heather looked away and was silent.

"Doug told me he would get some casts made of Vicky's teeth for Rick," Shari added. "I'll ask him to make one for you if you like. We could mail it to England."

Tears ran down Heather's cheeks. She just nodded.

Shari walked back to the bus, leaving her notebook on the table. Later, she returned to fetch it. Heather was gone, but a newspaper-wrapped package sat beside it. Inside were several small bones and the missing tooth.

"That's one mystery solved," said Shari to herself. "Poor woman. The temptation was just too great."

Whop, whop, WHOP, WHOP.

Excitement mounted as the helicopter lazily circled overhead.

Some volunteers ringed the quarry. Others, Willow and Victoria among them, sat on the cliff edge. Cameras clicked.

"Look at Mom. She rocks!" shouted Rick from the edge of the dig. He nearly burst with pride as Shari hung out of the 'copter doorway and panned her camera across the site.

Everyone laughed and applauded.

Marty, crouching by the plaster parcels, grinned and shot his wife in action.

Doug and the other technicians watched tensely. They readied the ropes on the plastered specimens.

A wire rope snaked through the air. Doug caught it, and he and Luisa hooked it onto the first plaster jacket.

One by one the gleaming white parcels were winched upwards. Like stubby birds, they slowly arced across the blue sky. The chopper slipped sideways and hovered over the truck, which was now parked above the cliff. Cued by Al's hand signals, each cast was gently lowered onto the flatbed.

Finally, Luisa and Rick sprinted round the bluff to the skull site. Doug was now on the cliff edge. He guided the helicopter's line and hook into the narrow canyon.

Rick reached out and caught it. It was heavier than he thought. He fumbled. The hook slipped and hit the plaster jacket with a dull thud.

He gasped.

"Don't panic. Try again," Luisa urged.

This time the heavy hook stayed in Rick's hand. He bent down, grasped the rope loops, and slipped them onto the hook.

Luisa checked that everything was secure. They stood clear and waved to Doug.

Doug gave the signal. Vicky's skull soared gracefully into the air.

Cheers erupted.

"Told you dinosaurs became birds!" sang out Doug.

The helicopter was finally waved away as Al and the technicians secured the plaster jackets to the truck bed. Everything was ready for departure to the museum.

"Clean-up time. All hands on deck, or should I say dig. Cold drinks back at camp as soon as we've finished," shouted Doug.

Wheelbarrows full of tools were pushed up the trail, and bulging backpacks were carried back to camp. Willing hands wielded the shovels and backfilled the quarry. Even Al, full of enthusiasm, came down and helped.

How would you fix up a dinosaur skeleton for a museum display? Real fossil bones are both heavy and fragile, so now it is usual to make casts of them to exhibit, while the real ones stay in storage where they can be studied.

Sculptors originally developed a method of making three-dimensional copies. A mould is made of the outside of the bone, which can be taken apart and put together again without the bone inside. Then the bone-shaped hole is filled with new material, which hardens into a replica of the bone.

The cheapest casts are of plaster of Paris, a white powder that sets hard when it is wetted and then dried. For display, fibreglass (which is light and strong) is preferred. Both can be coloured to look like the original bone.

Years ago, one dinosaur skeleton, a *Diplodocus*, was completely cast and copies of the skeleton were given to major museums around the world. Now many of the dinosaur specimens on exhibit in museums are fibreglass casts made in their labs. Other casts are exchanged between museums for research and exhibition.

www.i5ive.com/article.cfm/paleontology/46508

Finally, sweating and covered with dust, a smiling Jimmy and Wally triumphantly packed out the last vertebra. Marty followed with the camera. Rick surveyed the abandoned site for a few minutes, then followed. This had been the most fun he had ever had. Even if there hadn't really been a plot to steal Vicky, the spying had added spice to the hard physical work.

Willow and Victoria, engrossed in conversation, left Rick and headed for the rope up the cliff for the last time.

"I gotta go home," said an emotional Victoria. She hugged Willow. "Come to the farm as soon as you're dressed. Or want to borrow something fancy of mine? You can drive with us to the dinner." She ran off then turned back. "Here, I bought you this … for tonight." She dropped a lipstick into Willow's pocket then skipped off, turning to wave at regular intervals.

Willow waved and waved, then suddenly staggered as her head swam. "Oops," she thought. "How odd."

She started back to camp, passing the giant tractor-trailer. The huge white packages sat roped to the flatbed, looking like giant marshmallows. The thought of marshmallows suddenly made her feel ill. A shudder took her and she vomited by the truck wheel. She became aware that her head was pounding.

"Dad!" she shouted, scared.

Marty was out of earshot.

Dizziness swept over Willow again, and sweat coated her skin. She pulled her head scarf out of her pocket to wipe her face, then looked at it with horror. "I didn't have my head scarf on and I've got sunstroke and Mom warned me … I need shade."

Willow tottered to the shadow cast by the truck cab and leaned against the door. But even in the shade, the metal burned her face. She moaned, then saw the steps up to the cab.

"I can lie down up there," she thought, remembering the bed. Sluggishly she climbed up, struggled with the door, and crawled over the seat. She lurched over to the bed, pulled the curtains against the bright light, and collapsed on the narrow foam mattress.

CHAPTER THIRTEEN

"Rick, where's Willow?" Shari emerged from the bedroom, slipping on her earrings. "She hasn't changed yet."

"Last time I saw her, she was climbing the cliff with Victoria. Victoria was offering to lend her some way-out clothes."

Marty thrust his head out of the bathroom, towelling wet hair. "Uh-oh, borrowed finery. You're going to be upstaged, Shari." He eyed her blue cotton dress. "Shouldn't you be wearing skin-tight Lycra?"

"Ha ha, very funny," said Shari. She frowned. "Willow shouldn't have gone to the farm without asking."

Marty grabbed the cellphone and dialled. "Busy. Bet those girls are on the Net again."

Rick interrupted. "Can I go, Mom? Dr. Muller's offered me a ride. He says I can look at his fossil tooth collection while he gets changed, but we have to leave right now."

"I guess that's fine. Marty?"

"Have a good time, son. We'll see you at the restaurant."

Rick left in a hurry before his mother could make him brush his hair.

Dr. Muller let out the clutch and drove up the coulee. "So, Rick! Going to let me in on the game?"

"W-w-what game?" Rick stammered.

Dr. Muller grinned. "The business with the tooth. You're too smart to have dropped it in the middle of the trail."

Rick squirmed with embarrassment but decided to be honest. "It was a … a kind of test. You … you were a suspect. Because you collect teeth — like the one you showed me at your office."

Dr. Muller laughed heartily. "That would have been a nice bit of detective work, if I was the guilty party. There's just one flaw in your logic."

"What?" asked Rick.

"The tooth I showed you isn't a real one, it's a cast. Didn't you notice how light it was?"

Rick hung his head. "I'm … I'm sorry."

"So, are you pleased or disappointed the thief wasn't me?" asked Dr. Muller.

"Pleased," said Rick. "I want the thief to be someone I don't like."

Dr. Muller laughed and slapped the wheel. "Good point." He hesitated. "You might be disappointed in my real tooth collection. It's all surface finds, nothing as big and spectacular as the cast. But I do have a genuine *Albertosaurus* tooth."

"Awesome," said Rick.

An hour later, everyone gathered at Kwong's Chinese and Canadian Restaurant to celebrate Vicky's successful excavation.

Shari and Marty peered across the candlelit room, trying to spot Willow.

"No one from the farm is here yet," said Marty. He steered Shari to the back of the room. "Come and meet Bill Deeley and his wife."

Rick entered with Dr. and Mrs. Muller.

"Wow," said Rick. "I don't know anyone now they're dressed up." He went in search of his parents, waving to people he recognized as he squeezed past them.

The room became more and more crowded. It seemed as though almost everyone involved with the dig had come. Everyone milled around chatting, while the restaurant staff tried to encourage their guests to be seated.

"Willow's still not here," worried Shari.

"Relax. No one from the farm is. We'll save their places." Marty tipped up the rest of the chairs around their table to show they were taken. "Quit worrying and have an egg roll."

Waiters were serving the soup course as Victoria, followed by her parents, appeared at the door. Shari beamed and waved.

They bustled over.

"I'm sorry we're late. We waited and waited for Willow. When she didn't turn up, we realized she must have changed her mind and come with you ..." Mrs. Wilkinson tailed off as she saw the look on Marty and Shari's faces. "You mean she's not here?"

Shari and Marty leaped to their feet in alarm, and the room gradually fell silent as everyone realized there was a crisis.

Marty raised his voice. "Willow's missing. We need your help. Could we work out who saw her last?"

It took some time to confirm that Victoria was the last person to see her on the clifftop.

"Just a minute," Charlie stood up. "Willow's not the only person missing. So's Wally, Jimmy … and Heather?"

There was a buzz of conversation as the diners tried to make sense of this new information.

Doug stood up. "Heather, Jimmy, and Wally could have decided not to come, but Willow's another matter. We need a search party in case there's been an accident."

The restaurant staff looked bewildered as more than half the diners rushed out to their cars. Bill Deeley phoned the police, and Mrs. Wilkinson tried to comfort a worried Shari and a scared Rick. Victoria sat looking miserable, muttering about "the dinosaur's curse."

Shari suddenly stood up. "This won't help." She blew her nose. "Could we organize a command centre at the farm?"

Willow stirred. She was cold and still feeling sleepy, sick, and dizzy. Her head hurt, and the roaring noise didn't help. She was shivering so violently she felt as though the entire world was vibrating. She groaned, pulled a blanket over her body, closed her eyes, and wished she were dead. Despite her discomfort, she fell once more into a deep sleep.

The crew changed back into field gear and assembled by the kitchen trailer.

"Willow may have fallen. Let's search the badland coulees before it gets completely dark." Doug's voice was more forceful than usual as he sent groups in different directions. "Take flashlights for the deep shadows."

Marty and Al commandeered Doug's four-wheel drive. "We'll search the trail between here and the top of the bluff, and then check the farm tracks across the prairie," Marty said anxiously. The rope up the cliff was in that direction, and Bill Deeley's experience had been running through his head all the way from the restaurant.

"Willow? Willow?" Marty shouted, hanging out of the window and peering into the twilight. He was systematically driving 100 metres, then stopping to listen.

"Try the horn," suggested Al. Marty leaned on the horn. It echoed dolefully through the badlands. They both listened, but there was no answering shout.

Finally they reached the cliff. Marty and Al got out and peered down. The rope was still in place, and there was no sign of Willow. "I'm afraid we should look for signs of a struggle," said Marty.

"We're looking for more than that," said Al, staring at the dark empty field. "Where's my cotton-pickin' rig?"

The farm, as the nearest place with a reliable phone line, became search headquarters. An emergency meeting was in full swing in the kitchen.

Corporal Lacoste of the Mounties was listening to Doug,

Shari, Marty, and Al. His broad face with its big moustache bore a puzzled frown as he desperately tried to fit together the puzzle pieces.

The overwhelming consensus was that Heather, Jimmy, and Wally were a gang of three. They'd hijacked the tractor-trailer with its precious load and kidnapped Willow into the bargain.

Rick stood in the doorway and tried to attract his father's attention. "Dad," he whispered. "Victoria and I think ..."

"Not now," said Marty. "This isn't a game."

Rick tried his mother. He tugged on her arm. "Mom, Mom, listen ... I learned some stuff on the Net ..."

Shari patted his shoulder. "Rick, make yourself scarce. You and Victoria need to give us time and space to figure this out. Okay?"

Frustrated, Rick stomped out of the living room. "Come on, Victoria, they won't listen. We'll have to solve it ourselves."

They crept into the office, shut the door, and booted up the computer.

Victoria clutched Rick's arm. "You've got mail," she breathed.

Dear Mr. Van Bosch,

Thank you for your expression of interest in our *T. rex* and for supplying your credentials. The specimen may be viewed by your North American agent. It will be in a warehouse in Dinosaur, Utah, for five days only, from Saturday, August 27th. Please confirm with us by e-mail, and we will give you further instructions. We are sure you understand that this information must be kept strictly confidential.

Dinosaurs Unlimited

"That's tomorrow!" said Vicky.

"Print it out!" said Rick.

As the printer clattered, a furious Janet Wilkinson burst through the door, with Shari close behind her.

"Victoria, Rick! Turn off that computer immediately. How dare you tie up the phone lines. This is not the time to play games."

"How could you," Shari snarled at her son.

"No, no, listen ..." said Rick frantically.

"Mom, you don't understand!" shouted Victoria.

"You're darn right, young lady," her mom shot back. "Go to your bedroom."

"AAARG!" Victoria screamed with frustration, ran up the stairs, and slammed the bedroom door.

Rick looked at his mother's white face, snatched the paper out of the printer, pushed past her, and erupted into the living room waving it over his head.

"STOP."

There was dead silence.

"Listen. I know where they're going!"

"Where who are going?" asked the corporal.

"Vicky and Willow."

"Who's Vicky? Is she another missing child?" The Mountie flipped open another page in his notebook.

Rick rolled his eyes and thrust the printout under Doug's nose.

"Dinosaur, Utah. See … Vicky's going to be sold to a billionaire."

"How do you know?" asked Doug, turning his full attention to Rick. "Where did you get this?"

"In my e-mail," Rick shouted. "I'm the billionaire."

CHAPTER FOURTEEN

Willow woke with a start. Everything was gloomy. Where was she? There was a constant vibration but it didn't feel or sound like the engine of the family bus. And this bed wasn't hers. She rubbed her hands over her face and tried to think.

She remembered feeling ill … sunstroke. She'd needed to find shade. Yes, she'd climbed into the sleeping cab of the giant truck to lie down. She must have passed out. What time was it? Willow squinted at the luminous dial of her watch. 9:00 PM. WHAT?

The vibrations suddenly felt worse.

This truck was moving! From the way it was shaking, it was travelling down a gravel road. Someone had driven off in the truck while she was fast asleep. Should she call out?

But she was still feeling nauseous. The giant rig rumbled on. The flying gravel made so much noise, no one would hear if she did. It could wait until she felt a little better.

The atmosphere at the farm was tense.

"Let me get this straight," said Corporal Lacoste. "You

kids discovered that the dinosaur — Vicky — was being advertised for sale on the Web." He glared at Rick over his notebook. "Why didn't you report it?"

"There was no real proof it was Vicky." Rick shrugged. "There still isn't. Besides, who would have believed me — everyone knew Vicky was going to the Tyrrell Museum — even Victoria and Willow didn't believe me at first!"

"Know who's stolen it?"

Rick shrugged again. "Jimmy and Wally, I guess. Willow and I overheard them talking about how much Vicky was worth. But we never saw them doing anything else suspicious. Heather was the only one who did suspicious things."

"What sort of suspicious things?"

"Well, Victoria saw her looking guilty and stuffing something into her pocket one afternoon at the dig. Then Mom lost a tape and Heather turned up with it the next day. She could have stolen it."

The Mountie looked confused. "Does this have anything to do with the dinosaur?"

"Excuse me, Corporal," said Shari. "I can shed light on Heather. She stole some small bones and a tooth to send to her grandson in England. When I tackled her about it this afternoon, she gave them back." Shari turned to Doug. "They're safe in our bus."

"Thanks, Shari," said Doug, looking relieved.

"I think she left early because she was too embarrassed to face everyone at the dinner. Her plane leaves for England on

Sunday, from Calgary." Shari shook her head. "I don't think she's got anything to do with Wally and Jimmy."

"We'll check that out." The Mountie made some more scribbled notes. "Could Willow have gone with her for some reason?"

Shari looked confused. "I … can't imagine why," she stammered.

The Mountie turned to the truck driver, relieved to have a simple question to ask. "This rig of yours. Can you give me the licence number?"

When she felt a little better again, Willow's common sense reasserted itself. No need to panic, even if she had been kidnapped by accident. She realized she'd met the truck driver, and he seemed nice. In fact, he'd be the one who'd panic if she suddenly popped her head through the curtains and spoke to him — he might drive off the road. She'd better wait for him to stop. She would wait until the truck arrived at the Tyrrell Museum, then she could ask someone to contact her parents. They'd be worried. Willow settled down on the bed to wait. Despite her anxiety, she dozed again.

The truck jerked to a stop, moved slowly forward with another jerk, then stopped again.

Willow's eyes flew open. She looked at her watch — 10:15 PM. Panic swept over her again. This journey was taking too long and the truck was rumbling over very rough trails. She knew Drumheller wasn't all that far from the dig, and her mom had pointed out the route on a paved highway.

She knelt on the bed and peered out of a small, dust-spattered window. It was night, but the moon illuminated gently rolling fields. There was nothing to recognize, but it certainly wasn't Drumheller. Had there been a change of plan that she didn't know about?

Willow's stomach clenched and she suddenly knew. She wasn't being kidnapped, but Vicky was! So who was driving? Could Al, the nice driver, possibly be a thief?

The truck slowed at a corner, and over the grinding of gears she heard voices in the cab. She slipped from the mattress and tried to peer through a crack in the curtain. The passenger was just a dark silhouette against the glow of the headlights, but the driver looked familiar, with a big hat and a bushy beard. Even before he spoke, she knew it was Wally.

"Nearly there. Easy as stealing candy from a baby," he growled above the background noise.

"I won't be happy till we've made the delivery and we limp back into the camp in the morning," said Jimmy.

"Yeah, we gotta remember to cry 'cause we missed the dinner after our four-by-four got stuck in a ditch," Wally countered.

"And we had to sleep in it till it was light enough to find our way back," Jimmy laughed.

"And it's all true because the truck's still there," Wally added with a guffaw.

"Them nice Canadians won't suspect a thing," Jimmy said, adding thoughtfully. "Except maybe those nosy brats."

"Hey," said Wally, "who'd listen to them? Besides, it'd be easy to shut them up."

"Wally," said Jimmy after a pause. "You didn't have anything to do with Deeley's dive, did you? It sure seemed convenient to have him out of the way."

"Me?" said Wally. "Would I do a thing like that? I'm Mr. Nice Guy."

"As it turned out, we'd have been better with him. He was less nosy than the new lot!"

As they fell silent, Willow's mind was racing. She knew who had stolen Vicky, and it was a carefully planned scheme. And had Wally loosened the rope that dropped Bill Deeley down the cliff? If he didn't mind hurting people, what would happen to her if they found her crouched behind the curtain? She looked round for a hiding place but could see nothing. What would happen if one of them decided to sleep? If they came looking for something from the cupboards she could see around the bed? She curled up back in the bed and rumpled the blanket over her. With luck, in the dark she would just look like untidy bedding.

At last the giant tractor-trailer slowed and turned off the highway. After bumping over rough ground it eventually came to a stop.

The passenger side cab door opened, then slammed shut. Willow raised her head and found she was less nauseous. "Gotta find out what's happening," she muttered to herself. Talking out loud gave her courage. She got to her knees and peered out of the little window. In the glare of the headlights she saw Jimmy run toward a large barn and fiddle with the

118

catch. With a protesting squeak of rusty hinges, the barn door swung wide open.

Inside waited the blue cab of another tractor unit.

"They're going to swap tractors," breathed Willow, "so no one will recognize the truck. Sneaky!" She watched for a chance to slip out as Jimmy drove the blue tractor out of the barn.

Willow ducked down from the window, terrified someone would see her in the headlights. She peeked through the curtain. The cab was empty, and Wally's door was swinging open.

She heard the two men's voices and guessed they were uncoupling her tractor unit from Vicky's trailer. She didn't dare jump out when she knew Wally would have to move the tractor to make way for the new one.

And indeed, Wally clambered back to the wheel and drove Willow's tractor around in a tight circle. After he had leaped out again, she peeked through the curtain to see Jimmy backing up the new tractor. She realized they were using the headlights so they could see to couple the flatbed onto the new unit.

The driver's door was still open, and Willow crept forward ready for a jump. Suddenly, headlights shone into the cab. A new vehicle had arrived. She heard voices and saw a car beside the truck. The newcomer greeted Wally and Jimmy, and all three turned to the couplings.

Willow swung herself swiftly out of the sleeping compartment and eased herself across the driver's seat, keeping her head down. As lithe as a cat, she slid down the steps and melted into the shadows beside the barn. She was just in time, for as she turned and peeked, the third person turned and got back in the car.

"Shift the headlights round the back!" shouted Wally. "We've gotta change the plates and drape the tarp."

Willow crept forward. "If only I could get the new licence plate number," she whispered to herself. "I wish I had something to write with." She checked her pockets but only found the lipstick Victoria had given her. Willow grinned to herself. "Victoria said to use it tonight."

Jimmy, Wally, and their associate worked fast. Licence plates were changed and a blue tarp spread over the white plaster blocks. The rig looked completely different. The old tractor unit was backed into the barn and the doors swung shut.

Wally and Jimmy scrambled into the car, and the new arrival took the wheel of the truck. They all took off into the night, in opposite directions.

As the truck pulled past her, Willow scrawled its licence number in lipstick on the bottom of her T-shirt. Once again, she crouched in the shadows. As the hijackers drove off into the night, she began to shake.

It was the cold that finally made Willow move. A distant light glimmered through the dark. It was a long way off, but it was a destination in this unknown place. Willow jogged toward it over the moonlit field.

The farm dog roused everyone.

It barked and growled frantically, straining at its chain.

Willow stopped. "I … I won't hurt you, boy," she called, her voice uncertain.

Lights went on in the farmhouse, and a man appeared at the door with a shotgun.

"NO!" yelled Willow. "Don't shoot. I'm too young to die. I need help. Please help me."

"Sue Ann," called the man, "get yourself down here. There's a young gal outside."

Willow sat at the kitchen table, a blanket around her shoulders and a cup of tea in her hand. The farmer and his wife listened to her story in astonishment.

"So I don't even know where I am," Willow finished. "What part of Canada is this?"

The farmer slapped the table with his hand and gave a great guffaw.

"This ain't Canada, gal. They must have sneaked through the border somewhere, though I'd like to know how they did it. But this is the good old U.S. of A."

"Give over laughing." Sue Ann gave her husband a nudge. "Get the phone. This gal gotta call her Ma. Then you gotta get on to the sheriff's office."

With trembling hands, Willow dialled Marty's cellphone number.

"Dad," she said. "It's me."

CHAPTER FIFTEEN

e-mail from willow@adventure.net

hi victoria,
howz school? been in calgary for 2 days, and mom and
dad are busy doing the post-production on the film with
bill deeley. he's still got the cast on but he's feeling a lot
better. i'm still feeling a bit sick, and i had a nightmare
about driving around in a big truck with a t. rex at the
wheel, but otherwise i'm ok. any news about vicky?

willow

e-mail from victoriaw@alberta.com

hey guys,
school's ok, but sorta dull after the summer. glad you're
doing ok. we heard from the tyrrell this morning. vicky's
coming back soon. it was a big mess in the u.s. even the
fbi got in on the act. because t. rex is also found there,
the tyrrell museum had to prove vicky was ours. luckily,

our dinosaur is the only t. rex with young, so they have to give it back to canada. cool, eh?

victoria

e-mail from willow@adventure.net

hi victoria,
great to hear about vicky. any news about what happened 2 jimmy & wally?

w&r

e-mail from victoriaw@alberta.com

they're in jail in montana after the border guards asked questions, and the other guy is locked up in utah. doug says they should all be extradited to canada, but they're in trouble down there too because what they did was illegal in usa too. hey, think we'll be witnesses?

e-mail from willow@adventure.net

hope not. that would be scary.

e-mail from victoriaw@alberta.com

we'd be famous!!!! did you know there's going to be a fancy dinner at the tyrrell to celebrate vicky coming back?

V

The invitation to the Forster-Jennings family arrived later that week. "This is quite something," said Willow, a little overawed. She read it out to the rest of the family over breakfast. "They want us to have lunch with the director, then a grand tour of the museum. And then there's a party in the evening."

The party was held in the dinosaur gallery at the Royal Tyrrell Museum, not far from Drumheller. The huge hall was packed with guests, who chatted or gazed in wonder over glasses of wine and juice at the sculptural skeletons and models of the dinosaurs that towered above them. Along one wall, an enormous diorama showed skeletons of dinosaurs before a painted backdrop of them in life. Eerie sounds from the underwater exhibit near the centre competed with the conversation.

As Rick, Willow, and Victoria entered with their parents, everyone broke into applause. They moved through the crowd greeting staff and volunteers from the dig.

Corporal Lacoste, beaming in his scarlet tunic, brought them up to date. "Not really supposed to tell you this," he explained. "But the third partner was Wally's brother. He's the one who put up the money for the truck, arranged a place to show the dinosaur, and set up the Web site."

"How do you know all this?" asked Willow.

"Jimmy's started talking," said the Mountie. "He's hoping for a lighter sentence. He and Wally thought up the idea when they saw how good the specimen was. They had to steal bones and copy the plan to convince Wally's brother to come in on the deal and find them a client. They got worried by the filming in case it caught them out in something suspicious."

"What about Mr. Deeley's fall?" asked Rick.

"Officially it's still an accident." Corporal LaCoste dropped his voice. "But I wouldn't trust those two further than I could throw them. But I guess when your folks came in to finish the movie, they were scared to do anything else; one fall could be an accident, but two would have been too suspicious. But Jimmy says they did steal the tape and checked it out, and decided it didn't present any problems."

"Told you it was all connected," said Victoria smugly.

Just then Doug came to fetch them, his neat beard black and glossy against a brilliantly coloured Chinese brocade vest. Willow, Rick, and Victoria were shown up to a dais and welcomed by Dr. Jane MacDougall, director of the Tyrrell.

"Thanks to these young people, the Tyrrell Museum has its most spectacular find safely back in our care," she said. "The specimen is about 85 percent complete. Though an earlier collector seems to have found the lower jaw, Vicky is still one of the best *T. rex* skeletons to date. To show our appreciation for your work, we would like you to accept the following …"

The director passed out three cards.

"… lifetime passes to the museum."

Rick leaped on a chair and waved his in the air. Willow and Victoria did the same as everyone applauded.

Doug and two more technicians moved forward. They each held a *T. rex* tooth.

The museum director looked at the three friends with a twinkle in her eye. "One of our volunteers told me the cast of a *T. rex* tooth is highly prized among young people."

"I bet it was Dr. Muller," whispered Rick to Willow. He looked out into the crowd and spotted the dentist grinning up at him.

They were presented with one each.

Victoria stepped forward and gave a deep curtsy.

Gentle laughter rippled through the crowd.

"Thanks, everyone," Victoria said with a brilliant smile. "I'll be here every week to see what you're doing with my dinosaur. And I'm going to do some more dirt biking and see what else I can find."

She stepped back to applause.

Willow and Rick stepped forward next.

"Thank you very much," Willow said formally. "We are really pleased you got Vicky back, and it was exciting to be part of the dig and find the skull." She thought for a second. "Though not as exciting as being kidnapped with her."

Everyone laughed again.

Rick spoke up. "The tooth is great. It will be the best thing in my collection. And I'll use the pass as often as I can. Thanks." He pulled a plastic bag from his pocket. "And we've got something for you."

"You all know Rick and I use the Internet," said Willow. "That's how Rick found out about Vicky being for sale. Well, when we were on the dig, we discovered evidence that an earlier paleontologist had collected Vicky's lower jaw. There was some burlap and plaster ..."

Rick held up the pieces of burlap.

"... newspaper from the 1930s ..."

Rick waved a yellow piece of torn newspaper.

"... and a sardine can opened by someone who was left-handed."

She took a can in a plastic bag out of her purse and handed it to Rick, who mimed opening it with his left hand.

"So we checked things out by using the Net and e-mailing different museums. We asked a lot of questions," continued Willow, "and we've discovered who it was."

A ripple of interest ran through the crowd.

"The Royal Ontario Museum has confirmed that a man called Levi Sternberg, who excavated for them in the thirties, was left-handed — and he loved sardines!" Willow grinned. "He left the cans on every dig site. He collected a lower jaw of a carnivorous dinosaur from the same area and it's in their collection!"

"I think you should just ask for it back," Rick added. "Then Vicky would be even more complete."

The hall erupted in cheers.

AUTHORS' NOTE

The characters in *The Disappearing Dinosaur* are fictional, but the story is set against a real background, the badland areas of Alberta. The techniques of dinosaur digging we describe are based on the work of Alberta paleontologists, in excavations that David has worked on and Andrea has visited. And the story about early paleontologist Levi Sternberg is based on current research on the old sardine cans found at the site of old digs, and though the question is not finally resolved (scientists are a cautious bunch), they say it "seems likely."

In recent years, several specimens of *Tyrannosaurus rex* have been found in Alberta and excavated and studied by the Royal Tyrrell Museum. And since the sale of Sue in 1997, dinosaur skeletons have increasingly been part of commerce as well as science. Some have been stolen, others smuggled abroad, and skeletons have been offered for sale on the Net, so the events of the book are possible.

Earlier books in the Adventure•Net series are set in Ontario (*The Lost Sketch*) and BC (*The Silver Boulder*).